The Celtic C

Copyright © 2016 by D. J. Doyle.

All rights reserved.

ISBN-13:978-1519109453

ISBN-10:1519109458

D. J. Doyle, Kildare, Ireland.

No part of this book may be reproduced, scanned, or distributed in any printed or electronic form without permission. Please do not encourage piracy of copyrighted materials in violation of the author's rights.

Dedications

In memory of my mother.

Hope you enjoy

D.J. Doyle

Part 1

Chapter 1

A large crowd of mourners trudged behind the drawn carriage, like a dark wave flowing in a vast ocean. Lost. Two brown horses, with brushed manes, followed the dirt track to the burial grounds. They strutted forward effortlessly pulling the lifeless body of Aine O'Neill cocooned in a pale box made from the finest ash wood. It was noon, yet the sky seemed to darken, overtaken by the grey clouds. Bare soulless trees crept towards the heavens, and the air was stale and dusty. Aine's family marched behind.

"His second wife," an elderly lady in the crowd whispered to her unconcerned grandchild.

Tierney's first wife had died during childbirth four autumns ago. The fever became too much, and she passed away while holding and smiling at her new baby girl for the first time. Others considered her a fool to take on four children not her own, including a new-born. Be that as it may, she was a natural. Although not their birth mother, she had loved them and they loved her as much in return. Aine adored the children and pandered to their every need. Though she always wanted children, her health weakened over the years, and she was unable to carry an unborn child for more than a season.

Before they left home for the burial, their father, Tierney O'Neill, instructed his children not to show grief as it is a sign of weakness.
"Death is a part of life. It will come to us all one day," he said.

The children walked behind Tierney, gazing at the ground as they did, not wanting to make eye contact with the local villagers as they gaped at the unfortunate family with ominous faces. Leading the children was the first-born, the next in line to lead the clan, Fionn. Inclined to be brave and heroic yet cautious and a thinker. He resembled Tierney in many ways, dark hair and eyes, tall, broad and strong but with youth on his side.

Behind Fionn walked his brother, Brian, who was more like his mother with light brown hair and pale skin. Known to be timorous and unsociable, he never mixed well with the local boys. Tierney believed Brian was not quite normal in the head. Even with a stern face, Brian's teary red eyes were visible and, trying not to disappoint Tierney, he coughed out his whimpers.

The two little girls, Caoimhe and Aoife, held hands as they stepped on stones from one to the other. They wore identical tan dresses with curly brown hair and, as there were only four seasons between them, they mirrored each other giggling in their palms not understanding the full meaning of death and how this would affect them. They'd just lost the only mother they knew.

Aine brought the girls to bed every night and brushed their hair while telling tales of old, Children of Lir being their favourite. They screamed with excitement and fear when Aine mimicked the wicked stepmother as she turned the king's children into swans. Aine's long, red, wavy hair swayed across her pale and translucent skin as she played and laughed. It happened the night she became ill and did not put the children to rest. Their father was too distracted with his guests to notice what was wrong. Aine's heart ceased, and she died peacefully in her sleep.

Fionn reached out to hold Aoife's other hand. She was busy twirling ringlets in her hair. He glanced at Caoimhe and then Brian who admired his composed father and wanted approval. Fionn felt helpless to comfort them, life would ever be the same again for them. Knowing this, he did not want to experience the long grieving road ahead. While Fionn observed the mourning congregation, he caught sight of another entombment taking place. It was an unusual burial as one young woman stood there for this passing. Locks of dusty brown hair blew in the breeze out of an over-consuming hood of a dark grey cloak. Only moving lips visible. He was unable to hear what she was saying. Chanting of mourners enveloped him and became overbearing. Fionn stopped with this distracted and turned back to follow his stepmother's body.

Mourners stood silently when they reached Aine's final resting place. To watch the last bit of human contact she would ever have again. It took four men to carry and push her into the earth hole, dug freshly for the earthly kind. They were scrawny and seemed unable to lift a small bale of hay. Tattered clothes exposed inward stomachs with ribs and spines protruding from the thin blotchy skin decorated with scars from a whip or cane. As they mumbled to each other Fionn guessed their language from Gallia and knew they were underprivileged servants.

The local Father started his prayer to make sure her spirit journeyed to the heavenly place we will, one day, all go to.

*'May you follow the light ahead
When the path in front is dark.
May you always be,
In your time of sadness,
As tender as the singing of the lark.
When times are harsh may hardness
Never turn your heart to stone,
May you always remember
When the shadows fall,
You will not be alone.
May the light shine on you.'*

Heads laid low, hands held together, some ruffled with discomfort. They all had been here before saying farewell to a loved one with only memories now for comfort.
Then, just like the life left her body, the people left Aine and moved on. Now moving faster, the congregation steered away from where they had trodden in the clay to remember a woman they hardly knew and were quickly on their way back down the dirt track.

Fionn lagged behind out of curiosity of the lonesome girl. Strolling towards the other entombment he was now close enough to hear the sounds the girl made.

She was lamenting. Her voice was as soft as a fresh stream in summer, yet he heard sorrow in her tone. Tears trickled down her flushed cheeks, glistening in the little sunlight they had. He stood listening to her song of woe and farewell. Keela did not notice Fionn approaching. Now she felt his presence, he was close. Although anxious, she kept her gaze at the entombment and continued on in the memory of her mother.

As far back as Keela could remember it had always been just the two of them. Travelling, living off whatever faith brought them, which sometimes was just some berries from a bush. Her mother locked the wagon door when the men came to visit as Keela sat alone on the rotting rungs crying and then watching them leave, usually fixing the string on their slacks. Some showed interest in Keela, but her mother always insisted 'not yet.' Then she remembered those words she heard her mother say many times. "We're eating well tonight. Quick, get the mule harnessed up, we're moving on."

At other times her mother darkened the wagon and eerily placed candles below certain artefacts to set the mood for 'the work of the devil.' All knew them as the gypsy witches who talked to the dead, foretold the future and aided those who had been wrongly done by. Spells were a specialty; they were even known to work at times.

"Good day to you," said Fionn quietly, trying not to startle the young woman. "I am sorry for your loss." Keela did not respond and continued her lament. Fionn was able to see her face now and taken by her beauty. He studied her faultless skin, rich red lips and dark blue eyes that reminded him of a lake on a winter's day. Her hair a little unkempt and her hands dirty from burying the dead. It was not unusual for a family with little money to take on this duty. Fionn finally built up the courage to speak louder.

"I am Fionn, son of Tierney O'Neill, may I know who I speak to?"

Keela stopped, "I know who you are, I know who your father is," and with a whisper, "and so did my mother." Still, she did not regard him.
"Oh, you are keening for your mother? Please forgive my intrusion, I mean no disrespect."

Fionn awkwardly glanced away to see the grounds empty. Even when he craned his neck high, his family and the mourners were now out of sight. In his thoughts, he could not remove the image of this young woman's beauty. Turning to express his regret for a garish interruption, he now stared at an empty space. Keela was gone and had made her way down the hill to leave the burial grounds.

"Wait, please."

He followed in haste, walking fast at first, then darted as she was almost out of sight. Within reach, Fionn touched her arm, hoping to persuade her to talk with him.

"Remove your hands from me," Keela scowled.

"I mean no harm, I just want to speak with you," explained Fionn. "Can we meet again and start over? Maybe tomorrow. I pray you will,"
Keela halted and raised her head to glare into his eyes. They were gentle, his father's eyes never expressed this. Tierney O'Neill's were unkind with no emotion. Keela believed 'eyes were a gateway to the soul' and they were either open for all to see or closed with no way in. She feared those with the latter.

"My name is Keela. I will see you tomorrow when the sun is high in the sky on the road out of the village near the old church. This is where you will find my wagon."

Unknown to both, their rendezvous did not go unnoticed.

Chapter 2

Tierney sat at the head of a long oak table in the grand hall, prepared by the best craftsmanship and with the family for generations. Smaller tables surrounded them in a U-shape used by those of lesser importance. Leaders of every clan faced him, awaiting his acceptance to eat and drink. Tables were laden with the finest food and jugs full of ale, ready to be devoured. Tierney rose from his chair with his jug in hand and held it out high.

"To Aine," he bellowed.
Everyone stood up and lifted their jugs, "To Aine," responded the men in unison.

Then, like vultures, they hovered over their food before lunging into the feast in front of them. Tierney took no notice of their animalistic behaviour and pondered on his existence for a while.

Life had been harsh on Tierney O'Neill, and it showed. Scars from battles with rival clans were evident on his face. He towered over most men, and his arrogance intimidated all beneath his stature. Tierney spent many hours socializing with his fellow clan leaders, discussing political views, telling tales of old like his glorious conquests as a young man, and then later, when more alcohol had been consumed, the singing and brawling began. He attended these festive evenings to banter with 'the likes of him.' Now his mind thought of the two wives lost to him, no longer part of the living, yet still, he carried on.

The children would need another mother to take care of them, especially the little ones. Tierney wondered if it was possible to find another so willing to take on a full family. Friends advised him to choose a woman for what she can do for his family and not on her beauty as he had done before. Choices were limited for him now unless he chose to join another a clan from another province. He would need to make a decision soon.

Cathal, the personal servant of Tierney, came scuttling into the room lowering his head while passing the table of leaders, afraid to catch the attention of the strong brutes surrounding him and cowered as some roared with laughter. He did not receive an ounce of respect from the villagers and many times they would tease him about being a weak little rat. Cathal whispered into Tierney's ear, rubbing his hands in satisfaction as he did. With pleasure, he informed Tierney of the meeting between Fionn and the gypsy girl. Cathal stayed bent over and waited patiently for a response.

Cathal's terrible posture was a result of being the servant to the O'Neill clan as a young squire. Spending day after day on bended knee, waiting to be excused. Each time he scampered out of the room, Cathal was not brave enough to turn his back in fear of violence. His father had wronged the O'Neill's by selling them an ailing herd of cows who perished not too long after. They begged for forgiveness and offered their runt of a son to be the personal slave of the clan until his dying day. He lived in squalor in the stable at the edge of the estate and survived off the scraps from the O'Neill plates as well as the odd rat or badger as a morning feast.

Tierney, angered by the story he heard, squeezed his fist around the metal jug in his hand, making a clear dent of four fingers and a thumb. Betrothed to another, Fionn should not be with the likes of a gypsy girl. Word of this encounter would not be accepted if heard by his peers and he wanted to speak to Fionn without delay. He requested Cathal to summon his son immediately.

Cathal approached as Fionn checked the crops of wheat. Astounded and happy to hear his father requested his company while socializing, he followed Cathal back to the house. Had his father finally realised he was a man, not a boy, and should be by his side. Fionn held his head high as he entered, proud to be present with all the great leaders. Tierney finished his fifth jug of ale.

"Sit down here boy," demanded Tierney. "You did not return with your brother and sisters after the entombment today, you had me concerned for your well-being, where did you go?"

"I wanted to be alone for some time to mourn in my own way. I walked for a while and then returned home to do my chores," he responded uncertain how his father would react.

"You were on your own for a walk. You did not stumble upon anyone on your way?"

"No, Father,"

Tierney gritted his teeth since he knew this lie indicated Fionn's intentions towards the gypsy girl and it was not just a brief encounter.

"That is all, I will see you tomorrow."

Confused by the conversation, Fionn did not want to question his father after consuming so much ale and left without saying a word. Tierney beckoned Cathal to speak in his ear.

"Follow Fionn tomorrow and tell me what you see," Tierney scowled.

"Of course, I will watch them closely, Master," said Cathal grinning.
Tierney turned to his friend, Donal O'Connor. He had made a promise to him a long time ago.

"You are worried my dear friend, what is on your mind?" Donal asked.

"I don't want to say," replied Tierney, "It might anger you as it has me,"

"I am your closest friend and in some months to come, your family. If we are to have a secretive and untrusting friendship, I do not want my daughter to be married to your son," Donal said defensively.

"It is Fionn, he is taken with the gypsy's daughter and is meeting her tomorrow. I have ordered Cathal to follow and report to me if I need be worried, I will not allow my son to surrender to the enchantment of a gypsy girl. You need not fret, dear friend," said Tierney.

He did not believe his own words, besides one did not deceive the O'Connor clan and live to tell the tale. They were notorious amongst the powerful clans of Ireland and would violently deal with anyone brave enough to tread on their toes. A young man, who tried to scuttle away with one of their hens, lost both hands as punishment for his actions, which meant certain death when all their talent was to work on the land. No one ever set eyes again on the man who did not know who Donal's pretty wife was when he made advances towards her.

"I hope not, I have plans for our united clan to be the strongest in Ireland and if this young girl happens to ruin this, I will not be a happy man. You need to make certain this relationship does not blossom, and I know someone who can help with this type of situation," offered Donal.

Donal searched the table to find the person he sought. A grim man sucked on a pheasant bone and gulped down ale between every bite, Fintan Kavanagh. Tierney saw who Donal's eyes had settled on and was now hesitant as to how this conversation involved Fintan. He did not like nor trust this man and had reasons not to.

Fintan, considered 'impure' blood, did not deserve a place in his clan. His father, a madman, had forcefully taken his mother and was born out of wedlock.

He was not accepted by his grandfather Colm Kavanagh. However, being the only boy born in his generation, he took command of the clan after his grandfather's death. Colm's death was suspicious, yet no one dared make accusations.

Tierney believed, without a doubt, Fintan poisoned him. Colm had been a mentor to Tierney growing up since he lost his own father in battle against the English. He had promised to take Tierney under his wing and guide him to be a great leader.
Fintan put fear into most people by his wayward manners; he would growl like an animal and then laugh hysterically. Tierney believed Fintan took pleasure in the suffering of others and had no fear when going into battle. He would kill with no hesitation and no remorse, even women and children were not spared from the wrath of Fintan.

Donal waved at Fintan and invited him to join in the discussion. "We need your services Fintan, I know you'll enjoy it as it is known as one of your favourite pastimes." A gleam of alertness overshadowed the common unresponsive expression of Fintan.

"Fionn has taken a fancy to the gypsy girl. I know you were on familiar terms with her mother, who suspiciously died the other day. I assume you know who I speak of?" Donal raised his eyebrows, but the brute did not deny any actions.

"As you know, Fionn is promised to my lovely daughter Sile next winter when she is of age, and we do not need the likes of a gypsy getting in the way of this match. We need you to move this little girl along. Frighten her if you must or physically move her wagon to the next village. We do not want her to return. Do you understand?" asked Donal.

"Yes, I do," snarled Fintan. His eyes widened, and an evil smirk spread across his face. "I will see if Daithi wants to come,"

"So be it." said Donal.

Fintan and Daithi were two peas in a pod. Best friends growing up, they feasted on each other's immoral likings. Trouble sniffed them out like bears to a beehive and were known for their fighting skills and taking any woman they wanted. No single man was brave or strong enough to take on this duo. Weapons hung from their belts, two on each side; from a small carving knife to a large cleaver. Their use would depend on the circumstances and need. Daithi trailed around after Fintan like a scruffy dog waiting for scraps. Fintan made all their decisions, good or bad. He decided where Daithi lived, who he fought and what weapons he had. Fintan, feared because he was cunning and strong. Daithi, feared more because he did what he was told to do. An evil man is less dangerous than the man he controls. Tierney, although knowing what these men were capable of, did not utter a word.

Chapter 3

Fionn had awoken before the cockerel sang his morning song. His thoughts about visiting Keela later played on his mind and made him nervous, so sleeping was difficult. With a cloth and basin of water, he washed himself making sure behind his ears and neck were clean as Aine had always reminded him to do. Fionn envisioned her standing there, smiling while listening to stories of when he travelled with his friends, living off the land, hunting, and gathering. Fionn managed to master good hunting skills at a young age.

Fionn caught his first wild boar just after his voice croaked and deepened. He had carefully tracked it, from when the sun was high in the sky until it started to set in the west, studying its behaviour. Ever so slowly he crept up behind the rambling boar and with his spear raised, he thrust down and stabbed it in the neck, the blade piercing straight through to the soil

below. Blood poured onto the blade and down to the ground. The boar squirmed, trying to free itself from the agony while blood filled its throat and the squealing soon became a gurgle. Unable to run away and die in the undergrowth somewhere, it collapsed to the ground and accepted faith. It was the perfect kill. Feeling proud, Fionn carried the carcass home around his shoulders for his father to see. His clothes were bloodstained as they should for a victorious hunter. "Good. Give it to the cook, I can invite the other clans tonight to feast on this beast, and I will inform them of your glorious kill." he said.
Fionn, still considered a boy, had a lot to learn about politics and leadership.

One story, in particular, Aine loved to hear and laugh about was the tale of Fionn and his friends tracking a young deer. Extremely hungry, they had not eaten a full meal for two days and were desperate for meat. An unsuspecting deer grazed peacefully, unaware of the camouflaged hunters waiting to pounce. It lifted its head every once in a while, to observe and then continued nibbling on the high grass between the trees. They surrounded the deer, hiding behind trees and shrubs not taking their eyes off their dinner. They crept closer and closer, with spears and bow and arrows ready by their sides, until they had every avenue blocked so it could not escape. Unexpectedly, a loud shriek of pain came from one of the group.

Cillian jumped up and ran forwards, screaming, holding his rear cheeks with both hands. The other boys watched him in awe, they had no notion about what happened. Focusing so much on the small deer, they did not witness the large stag approaching from behind. The stag shoved his large antler straight up the rear of Cillian while he bent over behind a bush. The loud yelp startled the young deer and stag. As a consequence, both sprinted away as fast as the wind. The other boys, shocked at first, could not help but laugh at their friend who was now wincing in agony on the ground. Cillian, unable to hike for at least half a day, swore to never be unaware of his surroundings again, no matter how hungry. They had no choice but to snare and cook some field mice for their evening meal.

Aine laughed so much when she first heard this tale and always loved to hear it again when she needed cheering up. He missed her dearly and longed to hear her laugh just one more time.

Soft stubble, barely visible, grew along his jawline and he wondered when it would become strong and harsh like a warrior's beard. Tierney had hoped, by now, the boy within would be gone. Fionn wanted the same. Dressed in his best clothes, and with the only pair of sandals pinched onto his ever-growing feet, he was ready. Still feeling anxious and uncomfortable, he played with his collar until it felt right.

The cook hummed a tune while preparing the morning meal for the family. Fionn sneaked up behind to scare the old woman as he had tried many times during his life. As he was about to grab her waist with a roar she calmly greeted Fionn.
"Good day to you, sir. What would you like to eat?"
"Good morning Kitty. Please do not call me 'Sir', I am not my father. There is no need to prepare food for me today. I will not be returning until sunset," Fionn said.
"Off out, are you? Who will be doing your chores today?" she asked.
"Brian has agreed to help me for today. I have told him what he needs to do,"

He placed some bread and fruit into a satchel for his journey. Caoimhe and Aoife came running into the kitchen and sat at the table observing Fionn's every move. Kitty placed full bowls in front of them.
"Are you going to visit mummy?" asked Aoife.
"No Aoife, you know she is with the almighty Lord now. We will see her when it is our time to be called to God,"
"When will it be my time? I want to see her now," being so young, Aoife questioned every statement and action.
"I explained this to you before the entombment Aoife. If you like, we can talk once more, when I return tonight,"
"Where are you going?"

"For a walk and that is all you need to know," replied Fionn. The girls, still curious, watched their eldest brother leave the house.

"Where do you think he is going?" Aoife asked her sister.
"I do not think he wants us to know," said Caoimhe.
"He may be going hunting with friends,"
Caoimhe disputed this, "In his good clothes? Not his friends. Maybe he is going to meet a girl!"
Aoife giggled, "Let us follow him for a while and discover the truth."

They gobbled up what was in their bowls, grabbed what they would need and ran out the door just as the cook served a second helping. Kitty threw her hands up in the air in disbelief and asked the dogs, waiting patiently at the back door, if they were hungry. Three gangly wolfhounds, with long sticky drool dripping from their mouths, followed the bowl's every move. They leapt into the air with excitement, their barks turning to high pitched yelps, as the leftover food was emptied onto the ground for them to lick up and bicker over.

Fionn's pace was quick to begin with as he concentrated on getting there in reasonable time. Tierney would not allow Fionn to have a horse yet, he thought his son too young to manage such a beast, so for now, Fionn used his legs to bring him everywhere.

The sun, still only rising, caused a pink glow across the eastern horizon. He thought about how he would approach Keela. Should he be distant and pretend she was just another girl or should he show interest and be polite.

"Oh, what am I thinking, just be me," he said. Fionn peeked around to make sure no one listened to his ranting, even though he knew only trees and shrubs were along this path. What would Tierney think of this insecurity, weak, he guessed, and would he approve of Keela? Images of his father's reaction appeared in his mind of when meeting Keela. He would see her as a rough gypsy girl not worthy to be part of his clan. Fionn, taken to one side and asked, 'What is the meaning of this?' What was he doing with such a girl?' He knew his father would instruct to get her away before seen by any of the villagers. He removed these thoughts as they would stir him up and spoil the visit in advance. Aine would have liked her. She was not judgmental and accepted people for who they were by their actions and not their upbringing.

Fionn squinted at the wagon in the distance on the side of the dirt track, all alone apart from the decaying church. The path continued on as far as the eye could see. He stopped and took a deep breath after such a long walk; the thirst became unbearable.

The sun, now high in the sky, beat down on him. Dark clouds were coming up from the south; a bad storm was on the way. Ever since Fionn was a child, he hated thunder, so he wanted to make sure he walked home before the worst of the storm hit the area.

Thunder always reminded him of the drunken episodes his father and friends had, pounding on tables roaring for more ale or slamming their jugs in a temper because of a disagreement. Being just a child, he would cower under his cover and tremble with each bellow or bang he heard. His mother would sometimes comfort him, stroking his hair, telling him it was a little storm and it would pass. He soon learned these were not storms when the screams came from his parents' bedroom next to his, yet the air was still outside.

As he neared the wagon, he could see the scraggy mule ate off sparse tufts of grass. Over the trees, the village was far away in the distance. Green mounds resided close which had many stories of historic duels and rituals. These occurred long ago and taught to him by his mother, a descendant of one the High Kings, Eochaid Mac Eirc, who died in the battle against the invaders from Greece. They fought for four days and, after many fatalities, decided to make peace and share this beautiful land.

Fionn caught sight of Keela through a small opening in the shrubs. She appeared so gentle and kind as she carried some water from the stream to the mule. The bottom of her pallid green dress dragged along the ground and dirt stuck to the wet cloth. A dark stain seeped up until a full ring of speckled brown surrounded the whole bottom of the dress and, with her muddy feet, her fair skin was barely visible.

The structure of the wagon decayed badly, the rusted nails that held it together flaked in the wind. Simplistic carvings decorated the base, mostly floral, and the wheels were missing many spokes. This wagon would not make another journey. A small fire burned outside with large logs placed over the flames carrying a steaming pot. Fionn felt hungry as the smell of food wafted towards him; a rabbit stew. He wondered how such a gentle girl could snare, kill and gut an animal.

Fionn cleared his throat and called out to alert Keela of his presence so as not to startle her. She glanced and then turned her back to climb the steps into the wagon, leaving the cabin door ajar behind her. Fionn could see her moving about inside and questioned why she did not welcome him. The rungs creaked as he stood on them to gently push the door open. "Hello," he said, still confused as to why Keela had not made any effort to acknowledge his presence.

"Come in if you are going to," she replied, "Can I get you a drink?"

"Yes, please. I am thirsty after the walk here,"

Fionn stared at Keela, hoping to make eye contact. Walking forward, he hunched over to not lose parts of his scalp along the sharp splinters above from the collapsing roof. It was a basic dwelling with little room to move. Shelves on one side carried, what he thought were, potions stacked side by side in slim glass jars. Some contained animal or insect parts. Another shelf held wax sticks of all sizes and colours. The other side had everyday utensils, jugs, bowls and some food, mostly potatoes. At the back was the seating and sleeping area. Trinkets dangled around his head; he recognised one of them as a gem to ward off evil spirits. Fionn did not believe in such witchcraft. He rested on a rickety wooden chair with worn material covering the arms and back. It was unstable, and he shifted nervously to ensure to even his weight. Keela spun around when she heard a loud crack.

"Nay, nay, not there, it's my mother's chair!" she roared.
She darted over, pushed Fionn aside, and pointed to another chair much stronger and more stable. Blood rushed to his cheeks, and he wiped the sweat from his forehead.

"Please forgive me, I did not know the chair was weak and belonged to your mother," the apology was sincere.

"You were not to know," she said as she saw the heartfelt expression of regret across his face. "So, Fionn O'Neill, what is it you want with me? Did you walk a long way to sit here and watch me do my daily chores?" asked Keela.

"I am here because I would like to know you. You have already stolen my heart with one glance."

She giggled, "Does your father know you are here, Fionn? I do not believe so. You say I have stolen your heart, yet you do not know me. This first glance you speak of, I stood at my mother's entombment, and I was melancholy. I do not think you know why you are here," she said.

"Maybe not, but instinct brought me here. I follow my instinct, and it told me to talk to you, and it also made me get up early and come here today, just to see you. I think that counts. I feel special inside when you are around, I believe our paths were meant to cross," said Fionn.

Keela gazed closely into his eyes; she believed he was being truthful. A silver pendant around her neck caught his attention, and he took the opportunity to change the conversation by inquiring about it, "A beautiful necklace, unusual. May I ask what it means?"

"It's my mother's, she said it has powers. It is a, em, Leprechaun staff, I believe. It has the power to protect against evil spirits. Unless the evil is within, then it becomes a host for it,"

Fionn comforted Keela, "This will not be your worry then, you are not evil."

Keela smiled and reached her hand out to him. Fionn trembled with anticipation as she touched his face with the back of her hand and moved it down to his neck and onto his chest where she turned her hand forward and rested it over his heart. She felt it beat fast, and his skin moist.

He wanted to kiss her, to move his lips over her neck and down to her chest as her hand had done to him. He bent down closer to her face. Their lips were not touching, but they were ready to embrace passionately.

Behind them, the rickety chair snapped and fell backward. Fionn and Keela leapt with fright. She backed away from Fionn and picked up the chair. Although he did not see her face, he knew her eyes were burdened with tears. Keela tasted the fluids in the back of her throat, it filled up so she closed her eyes to stop her tears flowing. She took a deep breath and walked to the other end of the wagon.

"Are you okay, Keela?"

"Yes, I am. It is a sign you know. You may feel we were meant to meet yet my mother is warning me otherwise. We are not meant to be,"

"Do you really believe that? It is an old chair I sat on and damaged, not a sign of some sort."
Fionn, now saddened and discouraged, slumped down on the side of a cot and gaped at the floor, "I cannot make you want me instead I can give you time to see me for the good man I am. I will not give up on us yet,"

Keela felt sorry for her hasty decision, "We will wait and see,"
They talked for a while longer, yet his thoughts were on the storm, his must leave soon before the storm grew closer. He told Keela of his quiet brother who only liked to play on his own, his two sisters who were always naughty when together. How he missed Aine and how he was concerned for his younger siblings being without a mother with only his stern father to guide them in the ways of the world.

"It will not take long for your father to find a new wife."

Keela's anecdotes were much more interesting. With her mother and mule, she travelled around Ireland to many villages and had seen many people seeking out her mother for a spell to help their crop grow or strike revenge on their enemies. Her mother had made a good living from it and taught Keela all she knew. She did not mention the drunken men who visited her mother daily, the men who did not request a spell or want to be told their future. Fionn listened intently and enjoyed the story of a village outcast called Thomas.

"This man was always drunk. Having lived a life of scrounging and begging, he stole from anywhere and anyone. Thomas staggered up to the wagon one evening and banged on the wagon door, shouting for mother. He wanted a spell to make him wealthy. Knowing this man's reputation, mother demanded the money first. Throwing some coins in the bowl, he sat down and waited. As my mother turned to get the instruments needed for the spell, Thomas had already taken his money back and some more with it. He had now become wealthier than when he arrived. She turned back and, holding a lit wax stick in her hand, she fanned dark smoke towards Thomas. The smoke surrounded him, and he started to cough heavily. Mother chanted a jinx, whispering as she said it:

'Money, may it come to you
Only if the source is true,
May you be enriched on this day,
If no harming of one on your way
This you seek, so may it be
To be punished if you take thee.'

"Thomas stood up and left without saying another word, happy with the thought he would be better off than before. He did not get too far when the stolen coins in his garments fell to the earth through a newly gaping hole in his trousers. As he tried to pick them up the silly man lost his balance and stumbled into a bush of thorns and winced with pain. He crawled out and made his way back to the coins only to be urinated on by the wandering mule. Groaning with disgust he tried to pick up the coins again. The slippery fingers of Thomas could not grab hold of them; he scraped the ground, but still could not grip them. On his knees and burrowing into the dirt with aggression the coins did not move and remained on the ground. He roared into the air and faced the wagon in the distance. 'You evil gypsy witch, you did this,' Mother just laughed at him. Thomas walked towards the village, mumbling. The story is still known to the locals of the ill-fated Thomas. Every time he tried to steal money or property some unfortunate event would happen to him, and he ended up the village idiot. Little did Thomas know; great wealth would be bestowed upon him if only he would change his unruly ways."

Noise from outside made Fionn leap up to listen more closely. Keela was more frightened by the abrupt jump than any disturbance outside.
"It will be the mule trying to pull away and gnaw at the shrubs," she said.

Shaking his head, he pointed towards the side of the wagon and sneaked out the open door, taking one large step onto the ground so as not to creak the rungs. At first, the bush rustled and moved beside the wagon, then Fionn heard a familiar sound. Two little girls tittered from behind the shrubbery, "Caoimhe! Aoife!" Fionn said in his most scolding voice. "Come out here now! What are you doing here? You could have been hurt or lost. You are both going home with me," Fionn was a little relieved, he now had the excuse to leave before the storm came, without being impolite. He would have liked to stay a little longer and share more stories but, with his sisters in tow, he now must return home.

"We wanted to see where you were going. Fionn, who is this girl?" Aoife asked.
"I will not be telling you, start walking home now, and I will follow. Wait until father hears of your long venture."
Aoife and Caoimhe knew they were in trouble, they sulked, swung their arms and turned towards the long walk home.

"Please do not tell Father. We just wanted to know what you were doing," begged Caoimhe.
"We'll see," replied Fionn. The girls held hands as they skipped along the road. They started to giggle and whisper again.

"Are you ashamed of me? So much you would not tell your sisters who I am," Keela asked.

"Nay, I am not. If I told them who you are, my sisters would not stop talking about me having a sweetheart. They would tease me,"

Fionn had been telling the truth, yet intentionally did not add they would tease him in front of his father. He would not tell Tierney about his sisters following him because he did not want him to know who he spent his afternoon with.

Keela held her head down as she was saddened to say farewell so soon; she enjoyed his company today. She did not want to be alone. Fionn moved his hand towards her chin and lifted her face. He gazed into her eyes and leaned forward, kissing her gently on the lips. He started to tremble again and pulled away in haste.

"I have much work to do on the farm tomorrow. May I visit you the following day, please? I would like to continue our tales."

Keela nodded and smiled. Fionn gave her a wink and turned around to follow his sisters with a spring in his step and a smile on his face. He turned to peek at the girl he was falling for. Keela watched Fionn walk away and touched her lips with her fingertips, wanting to hold his kiss forever.

In the distance, Cathal sniggered at the thought of Tierney's fury to hear about what he had witnessed.

Chapter 4

Fintan and Daithi started their journey at dusk, they had already spent their day drinking ale and were slurring their words. "The storm is nearing," Daithi said as distant flashes lit up the sky.
"Are you afraid of a little storm?" asked Fintan, laughing under his breath. Daithi grumbled, knowing Fintan mocked him, "This is good. It means we will not be heard."
They lit their torches when the sun had fully set in the sky and could no longer see the dirt track in front of them. The fumes from the burning oil consumed Daithi's nose, and he sneezed loudly, "Be quiet!" insisted Fintan.
"You said no one would hear us,"
"Yes, but we don't want to warn the young girl of our coming. I am surprised you did not go hungry when you were young with your rowdy awkwardness. The prey you were able to catch must not have had any ears,"

Again, Daithi grunted his reply. The rain followed them and soon caught up. It began to pour down. The drops were large and started to extinguish their torches. They held their hands over the flame and squinted as they tried to see the track with diminished light. The cold drops hit their hands with force and felt like little daggers of ice piercing the skin until they felt numb.

They rested under a tree to catch their breath they let their torches reignite fully by dousing more oil on the cloth from a bronze canister hanging by Fintan's side. A large flash of light bolted out of the sky and struck a tree close by. A crashing sound came from above, and the men thought the earth moved beneath them. The storm rumbled directly above them and being under a tree was not a good idea.

They moved on and quickly hurried to their destination. The flames reduced again. Luckily for them, the lightning showed the way for some time until they saw the wagon in the distance with the shadow of the old derelict church further on. They stopped to put out their torches in a puddle and crept closer and closer to the wagon.

Keela had settled down for the evening. The mule was tied to the sheltered side of the wagon, he had a habit of wandering off. She doubled the knot as the storm might upset him enough to run away.

Rain smothered the fire yet providing plenty of drinking water in the bowls she intentionally left out. Keela shuddered with the chilly air and blew out most of the wax sticks surrounding her. She carried one so as to see her way to her cot. All the trinkets clinked when she brushed by them. Her plans were to dispose of them and the wagon to anyone who was willing to own it. The mule would also bring a few coins to help with buying a small piece of land to build a single cottage with a patch of soil for growing vegetables. She even imagined being wed with children happily playing outside in the sunshine. Who would take on a gypsy girl? How far would she have to travel to leave the disgrace behind?

Lightning lit up the wagon and thunder bellowed above. Keela longed for Fionn to be there to comfort her. Her mother had always consumed too much ale to hear any noise at all, not even a violent storm could wake her though Keela still wished she lay in her cot now, roaring out pig noises and mumbling words.

The wagon jerked and the mule he-hawed. Keela peeked outside to see the mule gone. She quickly put on her cloak and walked to the back of the wagon to see if it sheltered there. Her feet sank into the soft, moist mud, and there was no sign of the dumb mule. She heard a tapping noise behind her, and turned to see an arm raised above her head.

Fintan clutched a burnt log, and with a heavy hand, he plunged it down on her. Keela staggered and felt the piercing pain in the crown of her head. The blood poured down into her eyes. Her vision became blurred red and then black as she fell to the ground with a soft thud.

The storm calmed a little when Keela awoke. She struggled to open her eyes as her lashes were wedged together with dried blood. Pain pulsed through her head; she felt every thud of her heartbeat. She tried to move. Her wrists were bound tightly around a tree not too far from the wagon. Sparks flew up into the night sky like fireflies dancing around before ascending to heaven and the fire flickered through the narrow gaps in the warped wood. The only home she had ever known, was now engulfed in flames. She struggled fiercely trying to free herself. Large drops of rainwater fell from the leaves above, she raised her head and let them fall onto her face releasing her eyelashes slowly, and they lost their grip from each other.

Keela glanced around yet could not see a soul and was confused. Noise escaped from the other side of the wagon.

"Who are you? What do you want? Let me go!" demanded Keela.

Daithi's head appeared from the side of the wagon and he seemed quite happy.
"Ah, she's awake. We thought the light from the fire might stir you from your slumber. We could not have you miss the remaining entertainment this night," said Fintan.

The voice sounded familiar, she heard it many times before and only recently just before her mother died. It was Fintan Kavanagh. The men appeared from behind the wagon, and she noticed one of them loosening his belt, as someone would do after a feast.

"You are a good cook, we ate the rest of the stew you made," said Daithi. "I now feel fully nourished,"

A loud rumble from his stomach escaped out of his mouth. Fintan and Daithi laughed heartily at the loudness of it as they strolled over to Keela and stood glaring at her. Keela sensed their intentions and started to cry, her fear grew, and she screamed.

"Please. Nay... don't do this."
Daithi instantly felt aroused by her fear. He moved towards her, then felt a hand on his shoulder pulling him back.

"I will be first," said Fintan as he passed by him and opened his clothing. Daithi, although disappointed, knew he would not have to wait long, he never did.

Fintan smiled at her crying eyes, she saw evil in his soul and knew her untimely fate was nearing. He slobbered his lips over her closed mouth and moved to her neck to have a little nibble of her young and sweet flesh. Hands fondled her breasts but felt unsatisfied by the tightness of her corset, so he grabbed the material tightly and ripped it open. Her breasts were now exposed to the cold and became rigid. Keela tensed and winced in pain as Fintan groped and squeezed them. Moving down he placed his lips over her nipple, playing with it. Keela could now feel the cold breeze on her legs. Fintan lifted her dress and cloak and pushed the cloth behind her waist where it was trapped between her and the tree.

No matter how much she struggled, Keela could not break free. Blood flowed into her palms as she twisted her fists around continuously. Fintan began to pant in her ear as he grew closer to being inside her. He tore her undergarments and forced his hand between the thighs to part her legs. She could now feel his ear on her cheek and quickly turned towards it. Opening her mouth, she took hold of his earlobe in her teeth and bit as hard as she could. He pulled away and instantly struck Keela across the face.
"Hell, that hurt. You, gypsy whore," he winced.

Blood consumed his hand as he held the torn ear and growled with malice. Keela spat out the chunk of flesh, and a spray of her blood covered the ground.

He was more forceful this time, grabbing both legs just above the knees and lifted them apart. He thrust into her hard, again and again. Fintan moaned with pleasure. Keela cried with pain.

"Ho, we have a beginner here Daithi," he shouted over his shoulder and then laughed.

He gripped the tree so as to give more force, then quickened and felt the tingle throughout his body as he gave his last few thrusts and ended with a sigh of relief.

"What are you crying for? Your mother never complained, especially when she was paid. Well, apart from the last time I saw her, that one did not cost. She no longer needed the money,"

Fintan winked at her. Keela frowned, thinking, trying to understand what he meant. It did not take long for her to grasp he had murdered her mother. She bellowed with rage, gritted her teeth and glared at the two men in front of her.

"Alas, this is not why we are here; your most recent courting is causing quite a stir. The O'Neill clan asked us to get rid of you, one way or another," Fintan laughed heartily.

It startled Keela to hear this and wondered why Fionn would do this to her. Did he want to use her, like many men with her mother, but his sisters interrupted? She felt betrayed and foolish to think that she trusted him,

"You lie. Fionn could not do such a terrible wrong to me," she growled, still unsure if this was the truth.
"You are correct. He could not do a man's work. That is why we were asked to do this," said Daithi.
Daithi grinned as he walked towards her. Keela spoke a spell of revenge her mother warned her would only bring evil and devastation. Only to be used if necessary, if no other spell would help, as the evil summoned during this spell seeks to own the caller's soul.

'Evil most foul, come from below,
To seek revenge on my foe,
Own my soul for this command,
So vengeance will be by my hand,
Curse the men, who do this wrong,
Curse their blood forever long.'

Daithi was inside her, groaning with satisfaction. Her nose filled with his stench and she vomited on his shoulder and rolled down his back. Keela repeated the curse again, much louder this time. Daithi wrapped his hands around her neck, not taking any notice of her words. He had finished with her and now came the part he enjoyed most. Fintan watched, waiting for the last exhale. Keela could feel the pressure on her chest struggled to breathe. She tried to gasp for air yet could sense the life slowly drain from her body. Daithi stood back and watched her head slowly fall forward. She was gone.

"A duty well done, I hope Donal and Tierney are pleased she will not return," said Daithi.
"This is not what we were asked to do you fool, we were meant to move her along to the next village and scare her enough that she would not return, so we need to finish by hiding the body," replied Fintan.

Throwing Daithi a spade, he pointed towards the small hill near them, "Bury her over there."

"I do not want to do it there. Where our forefathers fought for their titles? What is wrong with doing it here?" asked Daithi.
"The roots of these trees will foil your digging, and you cannot go deep. No one will ever realise she is over there."

Daithi sighed and followed his orders. He strolled over to the hills and started digging. The ground, still soft from the rain, did not take long to shift. He dug as far as his lower thigh and decided it was deep enough for such a small girl. Fintan snored and Daithi wished he slept beside him. It was a tiring day of walking, pillaging, and slaying. He awoke Fintan by kicking him in the leg, "I have finished digging the hole. You can put the gypsy girl in."

Fintan stood up and stretched, pointing his clenched fists towards the moonlit skies. He staggered over to the tree, still sleepy, and cut Keela loose.

Her body fell to the ground lifeless. Earlier he had taken blankets from the wagon to keep him warm while he napped and now would use them to wrap around the body. He threw Keela over his shoulder as easy as he would a slain boar. He held her legs and with one little heave he put her in the hole. Daithi stepped down into the hole and lifted her arms to fold them. She was cold now, and a loud crack filled his ears as Daithi forced the arms to rest on her stomach. With the first spade of earth thrown onto her upper half, it did not take long to cover the remainder of her body and fill in the hole.

Daithi searched the surrounding area and saw a large boulder by the trees down the field. He felt his belt to seek out a hefty blade and started chopping large branches from the trees nearby and sliced off the smaller branches. Daithi stopped when the large stack of sticks was sufficient, and he carried all of them in both arms. Placing all the branches in a row, he struggled to push the boulder on and asked Fintan for help.
"What is this for?" asked Fintan.
"To cover the freshly dug earth,"

They pushed with all their might, as it finally glided on the branches and pushed it up to the burial place.
"No one will be able to move this beast of a boulder and our secret is safe,"

When he fixed the boulder in place, Daithi immediately leapt back because a loud scream came out of the stone, "Did you hear screaming?" he gasped.

The storm swiftly returned, thunder bellowed above them. Clouds formed directly overhead. Lightning crashed down and struck him directly on the crown of his head. Daithi screamed in agony as the bolt continuously flowed into him and his body shook violently. Skin melted and peeled away from the burning flesh underneath and his clothes ignited. The bones in his hands protruded from what was left of their structure, and the tissue turned brown. Daithi howled as the flames engulfed his whole being and he slumped to the ground. Cries, now barely a whimper, ceased. Smoke from the carcass rose into a single cloud before being sucked down into a black hole in the ground made by the lightning. Fintan heard a slight moan as it disappeared into the depths of the underground.

Fintan reeled from shock at the sight of this atrocity. Quickly, he paced backward and stumbled to the ground, picked himself up, then ran away towards the dense trees and shrubs. Glancing back to see the remains of his friend in a heap on the ground, he could not believe his eyes. What was happening? He did not want to wait and find out.

He scampered blindly with no light to guide him, trying to avoid any rock or tree. A presence swiftly passed him on his left, and his heart raced with fear. Not wanting to follow in the same direction he quickly turned to his right and into the shrubs. A loud scream resonated all around. It was a pitch so high it penetrated his inner ears and caused him to crouch and cover his head in pain until it stopped. He crawled on his hands and knees through the undergrowth aware of the rustling noises behind him.

Another loud shriek rang out again, it was closer this time. He shuddered and froze, afraid to move anymore. There was silence for some time, and Fintan wondered if it was safe to come out. He listened for any indication to tell him he was not alone. The only sound came from local livestock in the distance. The first signs of daylight appeared over the horizon. Fintan sighed with relief.

As he stood up, a vision came straight towards him. Fintan could not make out what it was as he was blinded by the first rays of the sun. He shielded his eyes and expected the worst. The apparition disappeared, and a cloud of dust blew into his face. He instantly coughed. It was too late. The grains had been inhaled.

Chapter 5

Donal sat down to eat his midday meal with his wife Brigid and daughter Sile. It was a creamy vegetable broth, his wife was famous for, together with the soft crusted bread that soaked up the flavour. The secret ingredient was the right blend of basil, purchased from an English soldier, who said it had come from India, and thyme, the family's favourite. Brigid cared for the herb plant like a baby. It was rare in these parts.
"Can you give me some more bread please?" asked Sile.

Donal would soon be giving away his daughter, content she was joining a powerful family. Being young, barely out of puberty, Sile was growing into a beautiful woman. His son had moved on and given his lineage; two healthy, strong boys and another child on the way. As Sile was his only girl, he expected the same.

"I want you to meet Fionn soon. He is a fine young man, and the O'Neills are a strong clan, you will do well with a family of such good stature,"

Sile blushed, she had never even spoken to another boy apart from her own family so did not respond and continued to eat. Her mother frowned, Bridget was not pleased with Donal's decision and Tierney, with his brutish behaviour, was likely to ruin the ceremony. Instinct told her this was not going to end well.

"Leave her be. There is ample time for Sile to get to know her future companion when they are together," said Brigid.

Donal grunted, aggressively ripping bread with his teeth, unhappy with his outspoken wife. Brigid was blunt, and Donal did not appreciate her interfering with his decisions. Donal's father had arranged his marriage, and now it was his turn to choose for his daughter. Brigid would just have to accept his decision and learn to respect him.

It was noticeable how the years had aged his once striking wife. Dark hair now showing many grey strands and the lines on her forehead had deepened. She was still pretty, and many men would turn to leer yet when closer, time and childbirth had done its damage.

They had been together a long time, and she did love him once, but with the death of their little girl many seasons ago, Brigid never regarded Donal in the same way again. He was away, socializing with friends and did not return on the night she died. Having to deal with finding their little one on her own was devastating. Returning feeling ill, and with a head too sore to take in what had happened, he sneaked away to lie down and sleep off the effects of overconsumption. The guilt was there for how he had dealt with the situation. She would never forgive him.

Donal had been warned by some of his friends about Brigid, a strong spirit. She was never with her sisters and mother cleaning and weaving instead she was out hunting with her brothers learning the skills of survival in the wild. This type of woman intrigued Donal as he had never met one so sturdy before and saw this as a challenge. Brigid did not shy away from

Donal as she was angry at her father, he had forced her into marriage and wanted to confront the man who was brave enough to take her on. She could no longer be free to roam with her brothers and would have to stay at home raising children and serving her man. Brigid made many of the family decisions throughout their marriage. The village they lived in, the size of their house. When it came to the choice of who their children would marry, it was Donal who took charge.

The Flynn's' daughter was the first choice for his son as they owned plenty of farmland with many herds. This meant connections with the English and regular trading with them. This was a good selection for his son and improved his own status. Sile finished her food and left the room not wanting to be around if any quarrelling started. Donal and Brigid sat in silence.

The front door slammed open and hit the wall, the bang echoing throughout the house. Donal and Brigid were startled by this and paused for a moment, waiting to see who moved first. Donal grabbed the metal rod used to poke a dying fire and held it with both hands up in the air. They heard a scream from the hallway.
"Sile!" said Brigid.
They bolted towards the door. Sile was standing over Fintan, watching in horror as he tugged on her dress. He was trying to speak. Instead, the coughing and spluttering made it impossible to understand what he was saying.
"Let go of her!" ordered Brigid.

Sile was pulled clear of Fintan's desperate hands by her mother. Ushered to her room, she was instructed not to come out no matter what she heard. Donal bent down and lifted Fintan's shoulders.
"What happened? Did someone do this to you?" asked Donal.

He inspected Fintan. His eyes were swollen, red and full of dust. Around his mouth were large sores with yellow pus oozing out. Donal thought he resembled a disobedient servant he once dragged by a horse and rope through dirt and bushes, striking every stone on the way.

"G... g," Fintan spluttered again, coughing a black mass onto the floor before trying again, "G... gypsy girl," and closed his eyes.

"Get that dishonourable man out of my house. He irks me," said Brigid.

"Nay, Brigid. See the mess he is in. What normal man could do this to him? What if we have unknown invaders awaiting to attack. I need to find out his tale," Donal shook Fintan's shoulders. He was out cold.

"So you do not understand what he said?"

"Nay," Donal responded, lying to his wife. "As soon as he does tell his tale, tell him to go far away from here and never return to this house."

Fintan felt his inner nose burning and awoke with a jerk. Donal was holding a little canister and waving the fumes into his face.

"I knew this would stir you. You have been asleep for quite a while. You were shouting in your sleep. Now tell me, what happened? Where is Daithi?"
"Dead, he was melted into the fires below by the light above."

"What? Make sense man."

"She cursed us, she cursed us all," Fintan giggled with madness. The sun was setting.

"You are making the sounds of a madman," said Donal.

He grabbed Fintan by his clothes, shook him and pushed him away when the laughing did not cease. Fintan's movements became strange. Speaking clearly for the first time, the voice did not sound like his own.

'Innocence lost on the noble mount,
Where a touch will befall a wail,
A curse is destined on the line of men,
Only sacred terrain will end the tale.'

Brigid repeated the words he had spoken in her mind and wondered what they meant. Innocence lost? A curse? She demanded Donal tell her what he knew.

"Fionn had taken a fancy to the young gypsy girl. She set up camp on the road out of the village near the old church. I was not going to let her spoil the joining of our families. I gave the command to Fintan and Daithi to move her on to some other place. Instead, it is apparent they may not have followed orders and other acts happened,"

"How could you be behind such a horrendous command? That poor girl now seeks revenge on all of you and your male offspring. Oh nay, my son, my boy, my grandsons. You fool, you have cursed them all," Brigid sobbed.
Donal held his head low in shame and thought of his son and grandchildren.

Fintan laughed loudly with a high-pitched tone. Brigid cringed as the cackles became too much to endure. His body started to shake violently. Scrawny decaying fingers reached out of Fintan's mouth. He tried to scream. This time no scream came out, the obstruction made it impossible. Fingers clasped each side of his mouth and opened it wider and wider which caused the jawbone to crack and fall limp. The head fell back, and his eyes were directly facing Donal and Brigid, who was now screaming. Blood poured profusely as the skin on his face and neck tore open.

Two grey and tattered arms were now visible. As his body split open to the shoulders, the figure coming out wore a dark grey cloak and moved swiftly. Donal and Brigid could only see the back and dreaded what phantom they would see when it turned around. It wailed when it released itself entirely of the temporary shell being used. The sound was unbearable. Donal stepped back and fell over a chair, and a large lock of Brigid's hair started to whiten.

Brigid knelt on the floor, held her head down and covered her face with her hands.

The screeching filled the room, and it moved towards them. She could not bear to peek as she heard Donal howl out in agony. Blood splattered across her body, and she shuddered at the act being performed beside her, too frightened to move. Then silence. Brigid felt a wheezing breath in her ear. This unnatural soul was close, so close she could feel the blood-stained cloak brush her skin. Brigid believed she would meet a terrible fate there and now, instead she no longer felt its presence and a loud wail came from outside the house that caused the animals to stir. Brigid removed her hands and saw what was left of her husband.

Brigid darted towards Sile's room. She was curled up on her bed and leapt with terror when her mother entered, thinking it may be Fintan.

She was not given an opportunity to ask what all the screaming was about. Brigid was pulling her towards the back door with her cloak in her hand.

"Do not go into the front room, wait here. You must take a steed with haste. Go to your brother... Warn him. I will write a letter for you to give to him. Do not read it."

Brigid quickly wrote what had happened to his father and, as his male lineage, he was in grave danger. She also wrote the words Fintan had spoken before his demise. She prayed her son would understand what it meant and could be saved. Sile was hauled out to the barn, and Brigid opened the hatch to Donal's horse.

"This is father's horse, I can't take him. What has happened? Why do I need to go to my brother so late at night?" Sile asked.
"Your father no longer needs it, and you must give your brother this message. Do not stop for anyone and please be careful."

Her daughter was sent into the dim night lit only by a crescent moon. The village was in the distance, and smoke came from the flue at the O'Neill's place. She took a deep breath, lifted her dress to her knees and swiftly ran out of the yard as fast as her legs could carry her.

Chapter 6

Fionn was ready to rest for the night, he had worked all day on the land, feeding the animals and cleaning out the barns. Unfortunately, he had to bury the remains of some hens, attacked and taken by a fox. Snares had been set yet failed to protect them, and this greatly displeased his father. There would now be fewer eggs for their morning meal. Fionn was blowing out the lamp on the stand by the bed when, in the corner of his eye, he caught a glimpse of a figure swiftly pass by his room. Brian and his little sisters were in bed asleep; also the figure was too tall to be any of them. His father was drinking by the fire and would not be seen near the back of the house for quite a while. He poked his head out the door and glanced around. Not a soul in sight.

Tierney finished drinking his fifth ale by the fire. The heat warmed the whole room nicely, and his cheeks were glowing red.

He placed a hand on them, hoping to cool them down slightly. Only having put on a few fresh logs, they made hissing sounds caused from the damp within. Fionn had brought them in from the barn not too long ago.

Cathal's account of Fionn and the gypsy girl had rightly concerned him. Tierney hoped his son would see sense and not continue to visit her. He was convinced the gypsy girl put a spell on his naïve son. Had Fintan and Daithi moved the cart and girl onto another village? Guilt poured into his soul, she was only an innocent young woman. Outside, the hounds howled.
"Those dogs. Be quiet you stupid beasts," he growled.

They did not usually sound so fearful. He drank another mouthful of ale unaware two hands crept up the back of his chair and gripped it tightly before thrusting the chair forward. Tierney stumbled, head first, into the fireplace. His head hit the back wall with a loud crunch, the high flames scorched his neck and large yellow blisters developed before turning black. He was unable to react. Both eyes closed slowly when his head slumped directly into the fire, and the body twitched down to the toes. The skin sizzled and crackled as the fire engulfed his whole head.

Laughter filled the room as the phantom turned to face the trembling spectator in the corner, Cathal. He stood frozen for just a moment, then leaped through a nearby window and darted towards the barn. Horses neighed loudly, treading their hooves heavily on the ground, distressed by presence outside the barn. Crawling along the back of the stables Cathal hid in the corner behind some hay. With knees curled up into his chest, he whimpered like a baby. He heard rustling noises coming from inside the barn. Too fearful to view over the stack of hay in front, Cathal remained still. A pitchfork came hurtling through the stack and pierced his chest and neck. Blood poured from the puncture wounds, his clothing now turning dark red. The fork was lodged into the wood behind him. It would not come free no matter how much he struggled with it. Cathal's vision became unclear, but he was able to see the ghastly figure soaring above him and screamed, terrified, before his head fell forward lifelessly.

The large front door pushed open, a cold draught disturbed the fire and the flamed flickered. Brigid was panting heavily and bent over to catch her breath. Two feet stuck out through the legs of the chair that lay on its side. She slowly crept onwards and saw the body of the strong and powerful Tierney O'Neill lying down motionless. Where once a stern head was now just a burning skull with blackened skin melted onto the structure.

Running to the back of the house, she came across Fionn's room and expected to see yet another horrifying sight. Fionn was sleeping peacefully.

"Fionn, Fionn, wake up, you need to get out of here this very moment,"

"Huh! What? Get out of where? Is Donal hurt?" Fionn replied, rubbing his eyes.
She heaved at his arm until the dazed Fionn was standing up, "Your father has been killed, you will be next if you do not leave… and take your brother with you,"

"Killed, by whom?" Fionn did not understand.

"I will explain later, you must leave. Go to the church and pray it cannot find you there,"

"It? Who? Who could kill my father?" asked Fionn.

"I do not have time to explain now, you must go, hurry,"

"Are we being attacked by a rival clan? I will stay and fight,"

"What seeks you will not fear any weapon,"

"What about my Brian and my sisters?" he asked.

"You must take Brian with you, he is also in danger. I will wake the cook. She will have to take care of the girls for now."

Fionn ran to his brother's room and lifted him out of bed to wake him quickly. He did not tell Brian the details given by Brigid.
The cook was initially unconvinced thinking Brigid had eaten those funny mushrooms from the forest, yet the fear in her voice was troubling, and she agreed to stay with the girls.
A loud screech of laughter came from inside the house. Brigid ushered the boys out the back and turned towards the sound of their hunting foe. As she entered the main room, the phantom hovered near the ceiling.

"Do not go any further!" said Brigid.

Tierney's sword rested beside the fireplace and she grabbed it. Wrapping a cloth around the end, she poured over some ale and put it into the fire. Flames glistened in the dark room as Brigid stood in front of the phantom who now wanted to kill her son and grandchildren. Taunting it, Brigid stabbed at the air as a warning.

"I will not let you take my family. You will have to go through me first."

The figure propelled towards Brigid and pushed through her being. Evil consumed her body, and blackness spread with poison to every vein pushing through her skin like an unstoppable flood. The agony and despair were unbearable, and she fell to the floor, dying in an instant.

Fionn and Brian passed the entombments beyond the churchyard. The phantom circled the gates, unwilling to pass.
Fionn was unable to see the figure under the flowing cloak, yet it seemed familiar to him.

"Who is it?" asked Brian.

The phantom rested on the ground and removed the hood. Fionn recognised who it was, "Keela, is that you?"
She was lamenting, and Fionn was being drawn towards her in a trance, enthralled by the captivating voice. Reaching the gate, he lifted his hand to open the latch. Instead Brian pulled him back.
"No, Fionn, stay away. Please come with me."

Fionn shook his head and saw the real horror in front of him. Brian tugged on his arm and led him up the path towards the church door. The darkness of night was starting to succumb to the daylight, and as Brian closed the door, Fionn gave one last glance hoping to see Keela. She was gone.

Part 2

Chapter 1

. . . "The Banshee, as she is now known to our family, took her revenge on our bloodline for many generations. As soon as the boy became a man, she would take her vengeance. Now, as the generations continued on and the blood mixed further down the years, her power weakened, her existence faded, and she became unseen. She was only able to wail at night from the dark side, waiting for the cursed souls to pass over before dragging them down to hell," said Brendan.

Little faces stared at the elderly man, rocking in his creaking chair, hanging on every terrifying word of this compelling story. The children shuddered with the eerie sound the chair made. Brendan had the antique rocking chair shipped over from Ireland many years ago when his uncle passed away and had worked hard on the restoration. His grandfather used to tell the same story to him as a young boy, so to follow tradition, he insisted on doing the same.

"Are you finished frightening your grandkids with all that nonsense, Dad?" laughed Sean.

"Nonsense?" he questioned, "I think not," A damaged hip stopping him from walking properly, so Brendan limped over to where Sean was washing dishes and he spoke into his ear.

"Why do you not take our family's curse seriously? I warned you, I warned you not to marry an Irish girl, like my father warned me not to. Why do you think my father moved over here to Britain? He thought it would keep the curse at bay, but he hadn't expected me to meet an Irish lass here. I didn't listen 'cause I was in love and spent my life with my beautiful wife. You two, on the other hand, didn't even spend more than two decades together. Had a kid and then split up. At least your siblings married British blood,"

He took a sip from his whiskey glass and cleared his throat, "I hear the Banshee at night and do not deny that you don't, I can see it in the dark circles under your eyes."

Sean paused, thinking his father was probably right. Being woken many times to hear a howling noise close by gave him many disturbed nights yet he always dismissed the idea of The Banshee. Common sense told him it was a dog or teenagers messing about outside.

"The bloodline could easily become stronger, and you don't know your ex's history. She could be from one of the other families. Are ye listenin to me? You just don't know what the Banshee is capable of. Revenge for an evil and heinous crime has the right to seek justified punishment,"

"I loved my wife too, you know, and I didn't know she was Irish. How could I? Not that this has any relevance to your story, nor would it have made a difference," Sean rolled his eyes up to heaven, thinking the old man was losing his marbles. What would be the likelihood? Could Claire be a descendant from one of the cursed families? he thought.

Brendan left the room in a huff for his afternoon nap.

Sean smiled at the children, now playing hide and seek with the seeker being the Banshee wanting to pounce on her victim. Each child screamed with excitement when they were found. In the living room, his sisters were playing cards, their mother's favourite pastime and the tradition for the family on her anniversary. Not being a good player, and always losing his money, Sean thought it best to do the washing up after dinner.

Kevin, his teenage son, was sitting in the corner on his Nintendo, playing some game that would inevitably rot his mind. Sean could see the fast movements of Kevin's thumbs.
"Kevin…Kevin!" he shouted.
Kevin came out of his zombified trance and smirked at the sight of his Dad in pink rubber gloves.
"You'll have arthritis in those thumbs by the time you're thirty you know. Get over here and help me, the dishes need to be dried."

Kevin reluctantly put down his game to lend a hand, "Dad, the story about the Banshee, is it true?" asked Kevin.
"Why do you ask? You know your Granddad he can be a little odd sometimes." Lately, he had heard his son wake up screaming from his dreams. Sean felt his heart pound a little faster and worried his father might be right.

"I had the same nightmare again, the one I told you about before. It's the same over and over again, but each time I dream it, I get closer and closer to the girl. Last night, I finally reached her,"

"Tell me your dream again, son."

Kevin took a deep breath, "I'm strolling through a big field on a stunnin' day and I see this fit girl sittin' on the ground pickin' wild flowers. She has sandy blonde hair and is wearing like a grey cloak. She's hummin' a tune and it's calling to me, pulling me towards her. When I get there, she stands up and goes to kiss me. So, like any normal bloke, I do. I close my eyes and snog the face off her. I mean kiss, I don't want to confuse you. Then I hear her startin' to laugh, a really high pitched squeal of a laugh. I move my head away and I see this rotten, old, fugly lady starin' back at me. I scream and go to barf and wake up, sweatin' buckets,"

Kevin waited for a useful response instead Sean didn't move his glare away from the kitchen sink, "Ah, it's just a dream Kevin, it's nothing to worry about,"

Kevin grabbed the tea towel to dry the plates and did not say another word. Sean felt anxious, was his son in danger? It was not too long before Kevin was considered a man and if the curse is real, his bloodline would be the death of him.

What did the dream mean? He repeated his son's description over again in his head.

In the back of his mind, Sean thought how much he didn't understand some of the words Kevin used and how the youth of today had diminished the English language with their street lingo and slang. What the hell did *fugly* mean? Even as a history teacher, he could not make sense of any of their text language; the Rosetta Stone was probably easier to decipher. Most of the grandchildren were getting ready to be taken home, it had been an eventful day of stories and games, and they were tired and cranky.

Brendan had come back downstairs, feeling refreshed and thirsty for another drink. Saying goodbye to all his grandchildren, he knew he wouldn't be around much longer to see them grow up. Kevin was the eldest grandchild and he did not know him at all. He had not been the best father in the world, yet he had mellowed over the years and could now spend what time he had left with the younger children teaching them about their family history.

The group stood in the hallway hugging and saying goodbye. As they made their way out the front door, each one of Sean's sisters lit a tea-candle and placed it on the hallway stand. This was to show their mother they always thought of her even though they were leaving the family home.

Now the only ones remaining in the house were Brendan, Sean and Kevin, three generations of the MacNeal family sitting together in the living room yet miles apart in their thoughts. Sean glanced around the room at the images of his family surrounding him.

A large picture of his parents, on their wedding day, hung beside the fireplace. Images of him and his sisters as young children spread across the walls and a few small wedding pictures on the china cabinet. One was with his ex-wife Claire, he remembered how happy they were and wondered where it all went wrong.

Sean decided to move back home after their separation three years ago. Sean and Claire had been together fourteen years and the arguments had spiralled out of control. It was hard on Kevin at first yet a peaceful house was appreciated in the end. Kevin came to stay with him every second weekend.

He still cared for Claire, yet the love was now lost between them. They agreed it was best to split before they despised each other. Kevin was grown up enough to cope with the divorce. There were other reasons to move in with his father, Brendan was becoming frail and could not take care of himself as well as before.

To his children's amazement, he had become quite self-sufficient after the death of their mother from breast cancer ten years ago.

'If only she had that lump checked' Sean always thought. The house was kept tidy and the bills were paid on time. He even vacuumed once a week. Everybody who knew him could not believe he could switch one on. He learned to cook his favourite meals, although frying up a few sausages, bacon and eggs didn't require much cookery talent but he managed. Brendan's downfall was the amount of Irish whiskey consumed on a daily basis.

A considerable amount of his weekly pension was spent at the local off licence. His wife, Deirdre, would not be happy about his spending habits. Their mother was a typical Irish mammy, rearing all the children until they were old enough to take care of themselves by cooking their meals every day, stitching their clothes when they were torn and even cleaning behind their ears during every bath time. Yes, Deirdre was an Irish mammy, she protected her children from their drunken father and nobody could say a bad word about her.

The last reason Sean had to stay with his father, in the old three-bedroom house, was to save money. He was making big plans for the future and it certainly didn't entail the situation he was presently in.

Not only did he fall out of love with his wife, he also fell out of love with his job. When he decided to become a teacher, he assumed the education system could be enhanced by teaching history to his students in an entertaining way they might enjoy and actually take in the information. He also naively believed if you gave respect, you would receive it.

Instead, last week he was suspended for a month for aggressively detaining an unruly and uncontrollable student. The young thug spent months, giving back chat, being disruptive in class and the final straw was the threat he made towards Kevin.

"Kill the pig! Cut his throat! Kill the pig! Bash him in!" was written on a note to Kevin. Sean recognised the handwriting. What irony; a child with no interest in learning could quote from a well-known piece of literature.

Sean hoped to save enough money to travel across Europe, Russia and Asia for roughly two years and settle in Japan to teach English for a while. Then save again until he had enough to come home. Whether it took four years or fourteen years, it made no difference, he was in no hurry, certainly not to a society where the youth ruled the streets and were out of control. The latest riots had just proven his worries.

Innocent people being run over, shopping streets and houses vandalised and an elderly pensioner snuffed out for no reason. He could not comprehend what was happening to the country they lived in. Maybe he would settle in Singapore for a while and see what it was like to live in a place with the lowest crime rate in the world. Happy days, he thought.

Brendan was holding a glass of whiskey and swirled it around, mesmerised by the motion, listening to the tinkling of ice cubes against each other. He wondered when Sean would be moving out. This situation was meant to be temporary and with the teenager coming every couple of weeks, bundles of dirty clothes, stacks of dirty dishes and an empty fridge was something he was not used to. This is not how his household had been run for the past few years and he didn't like being told what to do either, being the elder he deserved respect. Brendan missed Deirdre so much and thought he could never manage without her yet life goes on and so do we.

Kevin played his game mindlessly with the odd grunt of frustration emerging from his mouth. This was his first attempt at Mario on a small screen. It was his favourite as a kid. The game, a present from his Dad, was at the top of the selling list at the moment. Kevin found it difficult to concentrate and was unable to sleep for long; his dreams had become too unsettling. "Can I have some of your whiskey Granddad?"

"You want whiskey? Go and get your own," replied Brendan. A drink would have helped him sleep.
"Your mother would kill me if you had a strong drink, so no, you can't have one," interrupted Sean.
"It's bed time, young man. It's late and I have to be up early to take you to school," Sean said.
"... and no more of that computer console, you need your brain cells for learning tomorrow,"

"You coming, Dad?" asked Sean.

"No, I've not finished my drink. I'll be up when I'm good and ready. Good night and sleep well," replied Brendan.
Brendan said those words a thousand times during Sean's life, and as usual he would have a drink in his hand.

Sean yawned on the stairs as he anticipated a good sleep. The creaking noises from the steps had increased over the years. A long list had been written of all the items to fix in the house. A few nails in the stairs should do the trick and the radiator in the back room needed bleeding. The leaking tap in the bathroom kept Sean awake many nights. Annoyingly dripping all night long. Limescale in the water was to blame. Sean was not a good handyman, far from it. However, he had learned to fix many household issues due to the dilapidated house they bought cheap when they first married.

They spent nearly two years renovating it and when it was finished he laughed. It reminded him of the 80s film 'The Money Pit', on a much smaller scale of course but just as dangerous. Feet had gone through the upstairs floor on a few occasions, they had burst pipes, electrical shorts and other catastrophes.

With his toothbrush in hand, Sean observed his image in the mirror. The wrinkles had deepened on his forehead and the crow's feet, by his dark blue eyes, grew longer.
"Where have the years gone?" he asked, rhetorically. Bending his head slightly forward, he caressed the thinning strawberry blond hair. The grey strands were now visibly overtaking its natural colour. He really had inherited his father's hairline; Brendan was practically bald on top. He closed his eyes momentarily, from tiredness, thinking of the soft bed in the next room. As he opened them, he thought he saw a small dark shadowy figure darted past the bathroom door. Sean spun around fast. Lifting his head up, to stop the concoction of toothpaste and water spilling out of his mouth, he called out.

"Kevin, is that you?" He spat out what was left in his mouth after swallowing almost half trying to speak. Kevin's was lying on the bed, still playing the Nintendo, this time with earphones, "I thought I told you to not to be playing anymore computer games tonight."

"Okay, Okay. I get the message. It's off now, are you happy?" Sean didn't respond instead turned out the light.

Kevin lay motionless, watching the moonlit shadows on the ceiling. Afraid of the nightmares to come, he did not want to fall asleep so thought of his Nintendo to keep his mind occupied.

Sean fell face down on the bed, cooking dinner for the entire family had worn him out. It did not take long before both were fast asleep.

Chapter 2

Sean dreamt about a classroom full of faceless, noisy students. The whole room a blur except one person at the back of the room. She wore a dark grey cloak, faced the rear wall and laughed hysterically. He instructed the room of youngsters to be quiet. The laughing became louder. She was disrupting his class while trying to teach therefore he decided to confront this infantile pupil. As he thundered down between the desks, the classroom seemed to lengthen and it took longer to reach the back of the room than seemed logical. Finally, able to reach out and grab their shoulder, he heard a loud howl that stopped him in his tracks.

Sean realised the scream was not in his dream and leapt out of bed when he heard another howl coming from the back bedroom... it was Kevin.

He dashed down the hallway. Brendan struggled up the stairs as quickly as his seventy-year-old legs would let him.
"What the hell is going on?" asked Brendan.
He was out of breath and gripped his chest; forty years of smoking had taken its toll. Though he quit ten years previously, when the doctor warned him his lungs wouldn't take much more, the damage had already been done.

Kevin was spread out on the bed with his mouth and eyes wide open. A shadow swiftly moved across the room yet when Sean scrutinised the ceiling, he could not see anything. Brendan was now sitting on the bed trying to sit Kevin up.

"What happened boy? Are you all right?"

Kevin did not budge and just gazed into space. Brendan shook him by the shoulders, "Banshee," was the only word Kevin said.
Brendan turned to his son Sean, his face pale. Sean stood over the bed in astonishment, "Did he just say what I think he said?" asked Sean, not really expecting an answer.

"I fucking told you and you wouldn't listen. Our cursed bloodline has grown strong enough for the Banshee to form again, this means she has the power to physically touch us. Kevin is in serious danger."

"This can't be happening. It's just a myth, a story to scare kids... isn't it?" Sean said, Brendan was not impressed.
"Okay, so let us say it is true, what do I need to do to save my son?"
He noticed how much his distraught son, who had still not moved, resembled his mother Claire. She would never believe this, he thought.
"You need to understand the curse, to try and find out if there is some way to break it. My grandfather told me there is always a way out of a curse. You need to find the way out. Now it's time to do what you are best at... history and research," Brendan advised.

"Hold on, no history book contains information about ghouls or ghosts. So how do I research something that has never been recorded?" asked Sean.
"The internet will only tell you so much. Let me think," Brendan folded his arms and tapped on his chin, deep in thought, "I think you'll have to go to the source and search for old publications and you'll also have to talk to someone about curses,"

"The source! You mean I have to go to Ireland?" asked Sean.

"Yes, they have libraries over there too, you know! You need to get a plane today, this morning. I'll mind the boy here, I'll ring Father David and ask him to keep Kevin in the church, and hopefully he will be safe there until you find out more. Now go do what you have to do," Brendan escorted Sean towards his bedroom and ushered him inside.

"I'll go check the airlines on my laptop. I hope there won't be an issue booking a flight at such short notice. Then I'll pack a bag."

Sean was able to purchase a seat on Aer Lingus but it would mean leaving in an hour. He grabbed a travel bag from under the bed, the last time he used this was to leave his wife. His wardrobe consisted mostly of shirts, blazers and chinos. He owned just one pair of tight blue jeans, they weren't always so tight, and some sweat bottoms used for going on the mucky field trips with his students. He now had three changes of clothing folded into the bag. The last item Sean packed away was his laptop, so he could do some research while waiting to board the flight. A taxi was on its way, it would only be five minutes.

Sean begged his father to ring Claire and tell her Kevin was suffering from a case of the flu and it was best he stayed in bed for a couple of days rather than journey to home or school. He hoped she would not ask to speak to him.

"I'll ring you in a while, Dad. Thank you for minding Kevin, I really appreciate it," Sean checked in on Kevin one last time, he was still gazing into space.

He worried how Brendan would manage to get him to the local church, but there was nothing he could do now.

An impatient driver beeped his horn to let Sean know he was outside waiting. It was still a little dark when he opened the door, but some rays of sun escaped through the tall office buildings nearby. He closed the door behind him, inhaled and made his way to the taxi.

Without much traffic, the journey took less than twenty minutes. The driver did try to make conversation. However, Sean could not be distracted from his thoughts. His only response was to answer the question as to his destination: Dublin. It was about all he knew at that moment. He needed to do some serious cramming when he arrived at Gatwick airport as he had to find a place to stay and a list of national libraries. Of course, Trinity College would be his first choice. He did not expect the library to be fully open to the public, so was thankful he remembered his ID from work. It might come in handy in this situation. How he was going to research curses? Then it dawned on him, like an epiphany: 'Go to the source!' The fable said she was a gypsy girl, so it was probable the gypsies would be able to help him. Sean waited in the queue to check-in; he ruffled through his bag making sure he had his passport, wallet, phone, laptop and some cash.

He knew it was too late if he had forgotten anything.

"Next," said the handling agent.

The agent handed over the boarding pass and Sean initially thought 'no turning back now'. Directly heading to the departure gate, Sean was anxious and had little time to find a bed for tonight and do some initial research. He found a quiet corner, which was not being used, one gate down from the crowds of passengers waiting to board his flight. There was no time for any distractions.

Thinking it best to arrange his accommodation first he searched for low-cost hotels in Dublin city centre. Expensive rooms were out of the question as his credit card had reached its limit. There were plenty of reasonably priced hotels near Trinity College and he booked the closest one. It was now time to do some research on the Banshee.

After thirty minutes of scrolling through many sites, he was no wiser. Wikipedia said, at the start of their content, she is a young fairy woman aiding warriors in the battlefield. Then she is described as an old hag with long, grey hair that lured victims by placing a comb on the ground waiting for someone to pick it up. Sean was more confused than ever.

All the information did have something in common, she appeared and wailed before someone died, whether she caused their death or not, was not clear. He needed to deepen his research by locating old Irish manuscripts, most likely considered Irish Mythology. Even though this had become quite real for him, society would tell him otherwise. The information on documents in Wikipedia was a bit more useful. Plenty of details on old manuscripts in Trinity College Library, including The Book of Kells. The Royal Irish Academy library, on Dawson St, also had plenty of old manuscripts and books. The good news was the Academy was not too far from the hotel either. Sean shut down his laptop; he had enough information to start with.

The clock was ticking, they were all due to board in about five minutes. The airline staff arrived to board first. One pilot was a blonde woman in her late thirties. Sean couldn't help but appreciate her attractive qualities. Maybe it was the position of command she had over such a powerful machine or the way the uniform hugged at her waist accentuating her breasts. He saw her greet the other cabin crew with dazzling white teeth to complement her wide smile.

Many of the passengers queued in a long line. Sean sat back and wondered why so many would stand and wait patiently for so long when all seats are assigned.

With only six people to go through, he walked over with his passport and ticket ready for checking. Being too tired and nervous, he did not have the temperament to smile, instead he managed a quick 'Thank you'. After finding a small space to fit his bag Sean sat down and closed his eyes. He was not the best flyer, he didn't fear flying, he just didn't like it. When the plane sped down the runway, Sean gripped the armrests tightly and took a deep breath as it ascended.

A large man had sat next to him and rudely spread his arms and legs. A strong smell of alcohol exhaled from his pores, but it was from a hangover and not fresh, so Sean turned his head for the remainder of the journey. All he could think of was Kevin, questioning if Brendan would be able to protect and care for him. It was a daft rhetorical question. Brendan would give up his life for any of his family.

Time passed quickly and, as the plane landed, he hoped this journey was not in vain. A fierce cold breeze made him shiver to the bone. Now in Dublin, there was no guarantee as to what was going to happen. If he was able to find a way to save the life of his son, he would. He had a plan, but how would it play out?

Double-decker buses buzzed outside the airport, all going to the city centre and he decided it was better than a taxi. Being confined to a small space in a car with someone who may not shut up was not appealing, this way he would be able to keep to himself.

Chapter 3

"I never thought I'd have to do this to a sober person, but here goes," Brendan threw a jug full of ice cold water over Kevin which awoke him with a fearful jerk.
"What the hell are you doing? Where's Dad?" Kevin rubbed the water out of his eyes and lifted his shirt to remove the excess from his face.

"You've been out cold now for three hours, lad. Your Dad is on his way to Dublin to see what he can find out about this curse inflicted on our family and try and save your skin. I have to take you to a safe place,"
"He's gone where? Safe place?" Kevin asked. Totally confused as to what was happening.
"I'll explain on the way to the church. I'm hoping you'll be protected there for now. We can ring your Dad later to see how he is getting on,"

Earlier, Brendan had put a few belongings in a bag for Kevin to take with him and then helped him with getting dressed. Putting clothes and shoes on a growing teenager was not an easy task. A disgusting odour wafted out of his trainers and Brendan checked if something died inside.
"C'mon lad, help me out here," begged Brendan.

Kevin came around slowly, put his feet in his shoes and stood up. He was a couple of inches taller than his grandfather and there was some resemblance, the high forehead, strong nose and a dimple in the chin. The differences came from his mother's side, the dark brown eyes and dark hair, "Right, let's go. Have you packed what you need?"
Kevin nodded yet still wondered what the hell was going on.

Brendan phoned Father David an hour ago and asked to be there for him today as it was an emergency. They left the house and Brendan explained to Kevin what had happened during the early hours of the morning.

"Your Dad is as confused as you, but that doesn't matter. He needs to find out how we can break this curse. I've told you about this since you were a little boy. I wasn't making it up, ye know,"
"I asked Dad about my dream yesterday, but he told me not to worry. I think it was her,"

"Well, I'm telling you, you should worry. The Banshee put a curse on our bloodline a long time ago; her sheer existence is to seek revenge for what our ancestors did to her. This is why you need to go to holy ground; I don't think she can harm you there. We'll have to wait and see."

They left the house and Brendan guided Kevin down the street and around the corner. They were not too far now and he could see Father David, standing outside the gates of the church, scratching his head bemused as to what was such an emergency.

"Hello Father. This is my grandson Kevin. Not much of a believer I'm afraid. I hate to ask, but can he stay here for a while, maybe a day or two? I wouldn't ask but it's a matter of life or death."
"Life or death? Surely not Brendan," inquired Father David.

"If I told you how, you wouldn't believe me. So please don't ask. Don't worry, there's no drugs or gangs involved. Let's just say, he needs the Lord's sanctuary as only the Lord can protect him now."

They brought Kevin into the church, led him up the aisle and through the back door into the living quarters. It was a humble dwelling with white wood-chip wallpaper along the narrow corridor to the rooms at the back.

They entered a small bedroom with a single bed in the corner, folded neatly with brown woollen blankets tucked tightly underneath. The sheets were pure white and the frame black cast iron. Brendan didn't think it appeared comfortable. What choice did Kevin have? He probably would not sleep much anyway. The springs, compressing under the pressure, made a loud creaking noise as Kevin sat down. A dark brown desk with a matching chair was placed in the corner. They reminded Brendan of what he used as a child when he was in school, the only part of his life he wanted to forget. Although beaten nearly every day by the Brothers with canes, and sometimes fists, he never blamed God for their behaviour and his faith never diminished.

"Okay lad, I'll leave you here in the hands of Father David. He'll watch over you."

"What? You're not staying with me?" asked Kevin.

"Will ye take yer head out of yer arse? Sorry Father. Where would you expect me to sleep, on the floor? Okay, I'll stay for a little while and we'll ring your Dad before I leave. I'll check in on you tomorrow morning,"

They sat in the kitchen with a strong cup of tea from the pot. If Father David wasn't sitting there with them Brendan would have slipped a little whiskey into it. Kevin took out his phone and called his father. He hoped to hear good news to say he wouldn't have to stay in that claustrophobic little room for long.

Chapter 4

Sean arrived before the designated check-in time. A discourteous receptionist advised of a charge to check-in early. He did not like the idea of carrying his bag around all morning with him so reluctantly paid. The room was warm and cosy with a large brown desk, like the one he had in his history room at work, and a small flat screen television on the wall. He didn't have time to catch up on sleep; he needed to get started straight away. He took tourist maps at the reception desk and asked for directions to Trinity College.

He remembered his identity card, it may come in handy later. Hordes of people were on their way to work and he moved left and right struggling to get through the masses. He reached a large building with enormous pillars and wondered if this was his destination.

Two brown doors with black iron handles were open and inviting him in. It didn't take too long before Sean noticed it was a bank and not a college by the marketing signs in the lobby. Bank of Ireland was on every sign. Mortgages, Car Loans, Business Loans. Undeniably he was in a bank. As Sean quickly turned to walk out he bumped into a woman with folders held tightly to her chest and knocked her to the floor. Papers scattered everywhere.

"What the hell?" said the woman.

Sean held out his hand to help the woman to her feet. Her hair was a light brown, almost sandy, tied in a sloppy bun held together by a biro. She had thick-rimmed rectangular spectacles yet her green eyes were noticeable. Sean saw the beauty behind the geeky appearance, "I'm so sorry. Are you all right?" he asked.

"My report! It will be all over the place now and I have to hand it in today. Thanks a bunch," Sean knelt down and gathered up all the loose papers being careful not to dirty them. The woman watched, disapprovingly, as Sean stood on one and jumbled the rest into a messy pile. While nearer the ground he unintentionally eyed her ankles and legs. They were slim yet athletic and the pencil skirt accentuated her hips. Sean stood up and awkwardly handed the pile over to the woman.

"You know, if you had them in a folder, they would have been kept in order,"

"No shit, Sherlock. That's what I was on my way to get. Thanks for the advice," she said and stormed off through the other doors into the main room. Sean shrugged his shoulders and left. He continued in the direction originally given and from across the street saw a multitude of people, who resembled students, walking through large black gates. Without a doubt, this was Trinity College; he was sure this time.

A small archway led out into a large courtyard surrounded by buildings, old and new. He searched and followed the arrows to *The Book of Kells*. They kept this ancient book in the library for the world to admire. As a history teacher, the opportunity to see such a historical piece, was not one to miss. However, he needed to focus on researching a mythical creature who wanted to kill his son. Cobble stones covered most of the ground with a tightly cut lawn on the rest.

Statues and modern sculptures were sporadically placed all around. Surrounding the entrance to the library were plenty of tourists taking their senseless photographs of plain brickwork. When entering the old library, he expected the 'wow' factor, instead he was dismayed by a trinket shop with absurd fridge magnets, T-shirts and other bits and bobs. Sean then understood the overpriced admission fee to enter. "Just one? Nine euros please," requested the cashier.

"I'm not here to see the Book of Kells, I just need access to the books in the library,"
"It's still nine euros. You also need a reader's card to access any books in the library. By the expression on your face, I can tell you don't have one,"
Sean perceived him as the typical student, unkempt hair and clothes and unwillingly working to get himself through college. Sean grew impatient and didn't like the tone in his voice, not that it was ill-mannered, it was just not helpful, "And where do I get one of these cards?"
"In the Berkeley library, just over there."

He pointed to his left and continued scribbling on his pad in front of him. Sean didn't think a thank you was appropriate so left without saying a word. He was unaware there were two libraries in Trinity.

When he arrived, he was asked for identification to be able to enter which he did not have so was directed to another desk to request a reader's ticket. Sean presented his work identity card, explained he was over from a college in London and was doing a paper on Irish Mythology. After scrutinizing the identity card between them, and photocopying it, they provided him with the card. He did not mention his current suspension. At this stage, he was unsure which library he should be searching in and asked for assistance.

Fortunately, the Berkeley library was actually the place to start and Sean was thankful he didn't have to return to the other library to deal with the 'pleasant' cashier again.

Believing this was going to be a needle in a haystack, he hoped his research here would not be in vain. All textbook contexts would deem the Banshee as a mythical creature and part of Irish folklore, so his objective was to read actual accounts, or tales, of people's experiences. Sean asked the staff if they had handwritten manuscripts or diaries, which they did, some as old as 300 years.

Luckily, a database was available to search for keywords and cross reference the content in the section he wanted. Sean was amazed and grateful for this. He cautiously searched the word 'banshee'.

Three results came back. Two Irish manuscripts and one diary written by a woman named Elizabeth Dooley, obviously of British origin and most likely a descendant of the English plantations. He thought it best to read the diary first as Sean wasn't able to speak or read Irish, even with his ancestral background.

The closest he came to learn Irish was when he was a young boy growing up.

He was led to believe, by his mother, 'feckin eejit' was Irish for 'good boy', as his father had said it to him many times. Then he said 'feckin eejit' to a friend at school for getting a difficult question right. Sean received the cane across his hands and confusingly returned home to question what he had done wrong. Brendan heartily laughed until he received a clout on the back of his head with a wooden spoon from his wife. Brendan never called any of his children 'feckin eejit' again.

Sean carefully flicked through each page and learned much about the life of this young lady. Elizabeth started her diary on her thirteenth birthday, the diary being one of her presents, in the year 1827. She had one younger brother, who annoyed and teased her at times, and was well loved by both parents. She attended Trinity College to study Art History and followed on to teach the same subject there as an assistant to the lecturer. Her status did not aid her in any succession as she was a woman. She lived in the same house she'd inherited when her parents passed away and stayed there the rest of her life. Her brother contracted typhus whilst on one of his many trips to England on the ships to see his grandparents, probably by sharing accommodation with scores of filthy slum dwellers. He died soon after.

She never married and had help running her household. She seemed to be attached to her second cousin, Alfred, who visited her in Ireland many times, yet he stopped visiting once he was wed to Jane Brightmore. Elizabeth loathed this woman and ranted about the marriage being convenient due to Alfred's family running out of their wealth and needed to unite with richer families. A strong friendship developed with her personal maid, a young Dublin girl with no education or etiquette but quick-witted and sharp. Elizabeth seemed to admire these qualities. They spent a lot of time together and Sean believed Elizabeth grew to respect and care for Siobhan. It was obvious her accolades of this poor Dublin girl exceeded any employer and employee relationship. His suspicions were confirmed when he read that Siobhan had spent the night in her bed and continued to do so for many years. It didn't state what exactly occurred during their time together. However, it was apparent to Sean what had happened. He read between the lines.

After reading for quite some time, Sean grew tired of the day to day events Elizabeth wrote about and assumed the information he received from the database must be wrong. He scanned through much quicker now, not taking in the events, but rather just reading the words. Sean slowed his pace at quite an interesting entry; Siobhan had arrived upset after visiting her family.

It seemed to be a one day off a year employment. Siobhan continued on to explain about her cousin, he was being haunted and would die soon, just like his father had when he was an infant. Elizabeth refused to believe men so young could be married, have children and then all die the same way. Siobhan made it clear…the men of this family were expected to reproduce at a young age, due to the family curse. Elizabeth thought Siobhan was foolish to believe in such a ridiculous story.

Four legs screeched on the floor as Sean stood up from his chair, disturbed and engrossed by what he read next. Students giggling from across the room, wondering what the 'old man' was so hyped about, he took no notice.

'Siobhan enlightened me with the legend of the Banshee and how the family from her mother's side, for over five generations now, were descendants from a cursed bloodline. The Banshee would pursue the young boys who were becoming men and take their lives in vengeance of a crime committed against a gypsy girl. She did not know the full history of the curse, but remembered an old fable from her grandmother.'

'Innocent on a noble mount,
A touch will become a wall,
A curse on the men,
Only sacred terrain will fall'

Bewildered and not knowing what it meant, Sean wrote down the excerpt hoping it would make sense later. He read on for a few pages, but no other descriptions came up worth recording.

Now it was time to deal with the manuscripts in Irish. Knowing he had to seek some help Sean requested assistance from one of the librarians. Unfortunately, they did not provide this service. Sean felt a light tap on his shoulder.

"I may be able to help," said a young woman behind him. He didn't realise anyone else heard his request and turned to see the woman he had bowled over in the bank, "As long as you don't knock me over again," she said smiling.
"You would be willing to help me?" Sean asked, not entirely believing he would gain assistance from strangers, especially when their first encounter did not go so well.
"Well, I am at the end of my free period now, but I can meet you when I finish at five o'clock. I am doing an undergraduate Early Irish course, so this will help me too,"

"Do you not work at the bank across the road?"
As always, Sean hesitated being offered help from a stranger. He had been burnt before like this, and thought about what the catch was for receiving this offer.

"No, not really. They have a lot of old Irish documents they wanted to translate and filed away, so I offered my services. I only did an hour this morning and then had classes to attend. I have to go back now. You can meet me outside in the courtyard by the main entrance at five. Make sure you photocopy the pages you want me to review. You can't take those manuscripts with you," she smiled again.

Sean returned the smile. He was pleased someone was willing to help him and also delighted it was offered by a beautiful woman. "Thank you so much, I'll see you later then." She whirled by him and made her way towards the exit.

"Wait! My name is Sean, what's yours?"
"Alexandra, but you can call me Alex. See ye later." Within seconds Alex had disappeared through the doors and Sean remained gazing, not knowing what to do next.

Sean skimmed through the content of the pages and photocopied the extracts he thought might contain any reference to The Banshee. Altogether he copied about thirty pages, it did not narrow down the search since there were only twenty pages in each of the manuscripts. With the research out of the way, Sean had over six hours to kill and wondered if he had enough time to seek out some gypsies to inquire about curses. He was willing to try. He asked a student where he could find any gypsy communities.

"That's politically incorrect, man. The term is

'Travellers'. Jeez, what planet have you been on?" said the student.

Sean did not realise his ignorance and felt embarrassed. Never wanting to know the joys and woes of the outside world, he knew he had lived a secluded life. It was one of the many reasons his wife left him. She always said he walked around with 'blinkers on'. Sean felt happy with what he had and didn't need to know the tribulations outside his own circle of life.

He searched for Traveller sites on the internet and found several locations across Ireland. A long existing site in a place called Ballymun was his best bet. Studying a Google map, it did not appear too far from the city. Sean had no clue as to where it was and thought it best to get a taxi, he packed up his paperwork and shut down the session on the computer.

He hailed a taxi from outside the entrance gates. Sean explained where he was going in Ballymun. Raised eyebrows and an awkward forced cough from the driver worried Sean.

"I'll leave you outside, but you're on your own from there, mate!" he said.

The car was quite new and had tan leather seats, the smell was still fresh. His exposed lower back stuck to it making it difficult to move across the seat. He shifted to pull his shirt down and felt the seat. It was his mobile phone and must have fallen out of his pocket. Luckily, he checked what it was as his phone was a necessity while here in Dublin. He had missed a call from his father with no voicemail, Brendan disliked leaving messages. He decided to ring him back when he had worthy information to tell him. On his way through Dublin Sean realised it was quite a small city. After just a few minutes into the journey they were already out in the suburbs. Use of the bus lanes quickened the trip.

"We're here," said the driver.

In the distance was a large Ikea sign, some wasteland and the entrance to the site. Rows of abandoned rundown cars populated the area like gravestones. One was missing its wheels and raised up with cement blocks and another burned out with only the structure remaining. As he approached the open area he could see walls separating each individual lot. The majority of the lots had just one large mobile home. Some contained up to three smaller caravans. A chestnut-coloured horse with scruffy hair stood tied to a fence. Large eyes glared at Sean and half worn hooves nervously stomped on the ground.

The animal was well nourished as a large sack of potatoes and a bucket of water were close by. Sean changed direction so as not to intimidate it anymore. Broken children's toys lay scattered everywhere and clothes hung out the front of every home. A dog growled from inside one of the homes which caused rampant barking to come from all different directions.

"Wha'd' ye want 'round here boy?" asked a man. Sean glanced to his right to see a man in his twenties, dressed in blue overalls and covered in oil. The man waited intensely for a reply as he cleaned the oil from his hands onto a filthy cloth.

"Pardon!" Sean responded, not understanding what had been said due to the strong accent.
"I said... wha' de ye fuckin' want?" the man said more slowly and aggressively.
"Oh, I was hoping someone could help me. I am doing research for eh, I mean a study on eh, traditional Irish heritage. I am of Irish descent myself and I was wondering if there was someone I could talk to about the history of gyp... of Travellers. I'm, em, inquiring about stories that have been passed down from generation to generation,"

Sean waited in silence as the man had a blank expression on his face. He realised he had not thought this through. Why would a Traveller just 'help' him? A study was not a good enough excuse.

Sean's mind was racing. Trying to stereotype a culture he never heard of was not an easy task. A light bulb turned on in his head, "Are there any fortune tellers here?" asked Sean.

"Ahh, that depends on how much money ye have boy!" Sean understood the man this time.
"I can bring ye to the best in the business, but it's a bit of a fuckin drive an it'll cost ye,"

"Okay, I can pay. Where are we going?"
"To a little place out in Meath. I'm heading out tha way now so you can come with me,"

Sean hesitantly followed the man towards the vehicles on the site. All were nearly new cars, including two Mercedes and a BMW, parked beside two old minivans. Sean prayed he would open one of the cars because the others screamed 'death trap' to him. To his dismay the man walked to the small blue van with rust patches all over the body. He reached his arm into the open window and pulled the lever to open the door. It creaked as it opened and inside were frayed black 'plastic-leathered' seats.

A large Rottweiler stood up to greet Sean with a snarl. "Don't worry, she doesn't bite... unless I fuckin' say so. Isn't tha' right, you little fuckin' bitch. Michael's me name but you can call me Mick, what's yours boy?"

Sean unexpectedly picked up the accent quickly. He could understand a lot more of what was being said to him now.
"Sean, Sean MacNeal," and shook his hand. Then tried to wipe the grubby marks off onto his trousers.
"So, you are Irish then, well kinda," Michael laughed.
"I believe the Irish name would have been O'Neill and was changed over time for the British to understand," he responded, still struggling with the oily hand. 'Fucking Brits!! Sorry, I know you're from there. I'm talkin 'bout the Brits years ago, like,"
Sean hauled himself up and pulled the seatbelt over his shoulder. He could not find a buckle to put it into.
"Yeah, sorry, there's no fuckin clip for the belt. Sure, you'll be grand,"

Michael fidgeted with wires under the steering wheel until he located the two he was searching for and connected them together to start the engine. Sean started to panic.
"The fuckin ignition barrel's not working. I keep meanin' to fix the fuckin' thing," he then sped off down the road and onto the motorway.

Sean questioned what he was doing in a stranger's car not knowing where he was going or how he was going to get back. The dog kept his head emerged between the headrests and drool dribbled continuously onto Sean's shoulder.

Michael drove erratically, cursing other road users when they drove in his way on the road, causing Sean to grip the dashboard and seat with fear.

"So wha did ye come all the way to Ireland for? To get your fortune told? Like there are no fuckin fortune tellers in England. My brother, his family and a load of cousins live over there with fuckin hundreds of other Travellers."

"I'm also researching my family history," he knew this lie would help him a little.
"Are they Travellers?"
"I don't believe so. I just needed to get some insight into the Travelling community,"
"I can give ye some 'inshite' and tell ye one or two stories if ye want, while we're on the road, like. Would ye like that?" Michael laughed and bounced on his seat with excitement.
"Sure, I'd love to hear your stories," said Sean politely.

This was the exactly the kind of situation Sean did not want to happen whilst he was here. He didn't want to be 'trapped' in a vehicle with someone with verbal diarrhoea. He did not want to endure listening to a Traveller talk about local stories, old or new, that clearly did not help. He would have to grin and bear it, and maybe tune out if possible.

"I was over in England a few weeks ago for me Uncle Timmy's funeral and me wife was talkin' to me Uncle's Mrs. She complimented the food she was eatin'. Now Uncle Timmy was the fuckin King of the Travellers over there. He dealt with all police and media stuff, tryin to keep people under control, do you know what I mean like? He was meant to be fuckin clever. Well, she told such a story I nearly pissed me pants…He hadn't been well for a few days, at death's door like, and he was lying in his bed waitin for God to come for him. He smelt somethin lovely and realised it was his favourite food in the whole world… soda bread. The smell called to him, so he jumped up outta bed and strolled into the kitchen. Sure enough there were ten batches just lying there and he thought 'Ah she's made me last feast before I die, what a wonderful wife' and starts chompin on one of them. It was still hot and melted in his mouth, he was in heaven… before he went to heaven, like. Then he felt a hard whack on the back of the head, nearly fuckin knocked him out. 'Jaysus woman, what did ye hit me for? I was just enjoyin' this last feast you made me before I kicked the bucket' he said. And she replied 'Ye fuckin rat-arsed tinker… the bread is for your fuckin funeral'. The story spread like wildfire and we had such a great night. The poitin flowed like a river and so did the blood, we had such a 'brawl', do ye get it? Ball… brawl?" he laughed.

"I get it. It's a funny story all right," said Sean.

Although he smiled all the way through just to be courteous the story did interest him.

"Now I know they're not history stories like you wanted, but I thought you needed cheering up, you've a face like a slapped arse on ye. Do you wanna hear another one?"

"I'm hooked. Go ahead,"

"Well, this one happened on the way home from a wedding. We were on a hired minibus bringing us piss artists back to the site. Me brother was sitting in front of his in-laws with his wife. The mother and father-in-law were langers after knockin back many pints and then a few whiskeys,"

"Langers?" Sean enquired.

"Yeah, you know, pissed, drunk, langers! Anyway, she had an empty pint glass in her hand and puked into it. She was like a fuckin tap, you'd think it was pure alcohol coming out of her. So it was time to get off the bus, but yer man had to carry her off. Sure she couldn't walk straight and was like a pinball bumpin' of every fuckin seat on the way. He asked me brother to hold the glass until they were off the bus. So we were all off the bus and straggling around and shit, and me brother, for some reason, thought he could handle another drink and drank the fuckin pint. He then made a strange face while yer man said to him 'ye didn't drink that sick did ye?' Well I tell ye, he started hopping around like a fuckin rabbit on speed and ran over to a wall and started fuckin lickin the thing... to get rid of the taste, like. He freaked out and screamed like a baby and we all fell around the place laughing. Disgusting, I know, but fuckin funny I tell ye... ah ye had to be there."

Sean's smile was actually genuine this time, he had never heard a story like it in his life. It did turn his stomach a little at the thought of drinking vomit.

"That was a good one Michael, you certainly have unusual stories. I have one if you want to hear it. I don't think it's as funny as those but I think we all have a story or two in us,"

"Will it take long? It's just…we'll be there in about five minutes,"

"Five minutes is all I need, trust me, it's not as good as yours. I was in a nightclub taking a young lady out on a first date. She was a pretty woman wearing a sexy blue dress and high heels to highlight that curvy bum... eh sorry going off track there. This was many years ago, so smoking was allowed and the place was full of it. We just arrived and picked a spot near the dance floor and beside a group of single girls out on the town. I smelt smoke and mentioned it to my date. As we were in an underground club I started to feel nervous. I could smell it, but I couldn't see it. 'Maybe it's a joint or a piece of paper' I said to her.

She could smell it too. So, after taking five minutes to try and find the source, I turned to see this huge bouncer coming at me full throttle. I didn't know what was going on, or if I did something wrong. I nearly shit my pants with the fright. He started stomping on my foot, telling me I was on fire. I had stood on a cigarette that hadn't been put out and my trousers were slowly smouldering up my leg. I was the source of the smoke. I didn't even feel it. So for the rest of the night everyone who saw the show called me hot-pants,"

"Hot-pants, fuckin' gas. If you don't mind, I'll tell tha' one later to me mates over a few pints," he roared laughing, "You're right, we do all have stories to tell. Well, it's just around the corner now. Mamma Bella will be delighted to see ye,"
"Who?" asked Sean. He nervously shifted in his seat. What was Mamma Bella going to tell him?

When they arrived, a crowd of people, mostly men, stood around a field shouting and punching their fists into the air. Michael pulled up beside the other parked cars and swiftly jumped out whilst the van was still moving. Sean quickly pulled the handbrake to stop it rolling into the car in front.

"This is wha' I came to see, I have money on this. Have to go, can't miss it," said Michael.
Sean was unaware as to what was going on within the big crowd. He hoped it wasn't a vicious dog or cockerel fight.
"What about my reading?" Sean asked following him.

Michael joined the crowd without considering his companion. Sean, now standing behind Michael, was shocked by what he witnessed.

Two men staggered in a circle made by the crowd. Both were battered and bruised and blood ran down their faces from deep cuts around their swollen eyes and noses. They were bare knuckle fighting. The one they called Jimmy, the older man with bulging forearms, was less injured and continuously punched the younger skinny guy in the face. Each time the young man fell, he didn't stay down and he was straight back up again to the delight of the crowd. Sean etched his way towards Michael not wanting to be noticed. He felt out of place.

"Michael, I thought you were bringing me here to get my fortune told," Sean whispered.

"Yeah, yeah in a minute," Sean patiently waited as Jimmy grew tired and the younger man, he now knew as Finto, took control of the fight. Jimmy was knocked to the ground after just a couple of punches.

The majority of the crowd cringed in temper as they lost their betting money. Michael was excited and collected his winnings from a not so happy banker. Sean believed the odds must have been high on Finto and even the smallest bet would make a nice sum.

"C'mon now boy, follow me," Michael quickly pushed through the crowds and made his way towards a large field.
Sean caught up and they climbed over a fence into a large caravan park mostly surrounded by tall trees which caused a large shade across all the homes.
"Well, what did ye think of the fight? Good, righ? I won a nice sum of money."

"So I gathered. Why did you bet on the small skinny guy?" asked Sean.

"Finto? Cause he's me cousin and I've seen him fight before. He's just moving up in the ranks and Jimmy didn't know tha Finto has a lo' of stamina."

They wandered between the caravans. Some of them were small with children poking their heads out to see who the stranger was, the larger ones contained many more people also curiously glaring out of their windows. Sean felt edgy, this was an unexpected part of the journey. He had no choice but to follow.

Michael slowed down and instructed Sean to wait while he entered one of the caravans. Someone was tugging at the bottom corner of his coat and he saw a little ginger-haired boy, about three or four-years-old, pulling to get his attention.

"Mister, hey Mister, have ye any spare change?" Sean didn't want to cause a scene so scrambled a few coins together and gave it to the little boy.

"Thanks, Mister," said the boy.

He walked away counting the money and then bent down and tucked it into his sock for safekeeping. Michael said he could go in now; Mamma Bella was ready. Sean took a deep breath and walked through the narrow doorway.

Chapter 5

The mobile home was more spacious than he expected as he strolled cautiously down to the end where an elderly lady sat at a small speckled table. Sean was slightly startled by her appearance yet was unable to cease eye contact as she welcomed him to sit down. Her face, filled with wrinkles and deep crevices that could probably tell a thousand stories. Only five or six teeth remained in her mouth and they were brown, almost certainly from a lifetime of smoking and drinking.

"I'm Sean, pleased to meet you."

"Sit down son. I'm told you want a reading," said Mamma Bella.

"Well, yes I do, plus a little more," answered Sean.

"More eh! Well, we'll start by havin' a cup of tea. Here, drink this and leave a little at the bottom. The bit with the leaves."

She handed Sean a small cup. He didn't have time to sip like a normal cup of tea, so drank it in one mouthful. It was hot, causing a stinging sensation on his tongue and throat as it flowed down. Sean let out a loud gasp and quickly engulfed air to cool down his mouth. Mamma Bella giggled and picked the cup up.

"You really shouldn't have done it so fast,"
She examined the leaves, studying every grain.

"Okay, let me see. Ah yes, I can see your many paths. Let me tell you your past and present first. Then we'll talk about what the future has in store. Hmmm... Your one and only true love is no more. You're still connected though, by a child. You both love him dearly. This separation saddens you, but you know it's for the best. You miss her a lot, cause she was your best friend. You're ready to move on and I see a younger woman coming into your life. Now, what's next? Oh, your work life is in limbo. I see a lot of anger here but it wasn't your fault. This trouble made you to back off and you feel lost. Now, the future. I see you going on a long journey. Not for a little while though. You will go, just not yet. Wait. I'm getting a message. Someone is trying to contact me from the other side,"

Mamma Bella closed her eyes and whispered strange noises. Sean did not want to listen anymore; he didn't believe in messages from the afterlife.
What she said so far could have been a best guess by the wedding ring mark on his finger. Most couples have a child. The only point that stumped him was knowing he had to leave work and the reason why.

"I sense your mother is here. I see a D, maybe Debra or Deirdre, she wants to give you a message. She said trust your father. I don't know what it means, but she's come out of the light to be here. She is extremely concerned," she continued to examine the leaves. Sean was astonished to discover Mamma Bella was getting it right, "You're on a quest. She is warning of a lot of danger! A loved one is in grave danger." Sean's eyes opened widely, he was surprised by the accuracy.

"A young man? And I see a... a lady in grey,"

Mamma Bella stopped and put the cup down, pushing it away.

"You dare bring this wickedness to me. This lady in grey is dangerous, pure evil. I cannot tell ye anymore."

"I need to know more. Please, can you help me?" begged Sean.

"To help you, I need to know the full story."

Sean explained what his son had experienced in the dreams, how he had felt an evil presence. Also how his father had believed their family was cursed by the Banshee. She sought revenge on his bloodline.

"This is true. I can see this in your leaves. Your bloodline is tainted by history. Your mother is also fearful, she has come back from His place," Mamma Bella pointed towards the heavens and blessed herself, "to watch over you but she cannot protect." Sean felt a lump in his throat and tears built up in his eyes, "I also found some references to the Banshee in some old diaries and manuscripts this morning. I was in the library to do research, to see if I could find information to help me,"

"And did you?"

"A little. I found what seems to be a curse from a diary and someone is helping me later on to translate ancient Irish in the manuscripts," Sean showed her the scrap of paper. Mamma Bella pushed it back towards him and asked him to read it out. He assumed by her reaction she was not literate. Sean read out the words slowly.

*'Innocent on a noble mount,
A touch will become a wall,
A curse on the line of men,
Only sacred terrain will fall.'*

When Sean finished, he explained the story written in the diary and how he realised it was related to his quest. His beseeching eyes turned up to Mamma Bella hoping she could explain it to him.

"This is no curse. This is what comes after a curse," Sean frowned as he thought what he had found was the curse he was searching for.

"I'm sorry to interrupt, but are you saying this is not a curse?"

"Yep, that's what I just said, are ye not listening to me? This is like the get-out clause and you're lucky to have found this as the curse wouldn't be able to help you, whereas this is your key to unlock the secret of the curse. This is typical of the worst curses, 'cause it usually means death. Whatever goodness is left will always try to give the cursed souls a chance."

"So, do you know what it means?" asked Sean.

"Not a clue son, sure I'm no scholar. The only part I understand is…your son is fucked unless you can figure this out,"

"If you can't tell me what it means, can you give me any advice?"

"Hmmm, I can only tell ye what your mother told me. Your loved one is in serious danger and this evil will not rest until it gets what it wants, revenge. But I think you already know this. If I try and go any further, I will put myself in danger and no money is worth it. Sorry,"

"Thanks for your help. I'm just glad to hear I'm on the right track. How much do I owe you?"

"Well, I thought it was just a reading. I didn't know I had to connect with the other side and give ye lessons on curses. I'd say fifty should cover it,"
Sean didn't argue and paid. He thanked Mamma Bella again and left.

Outside Sean was surrounded by children. The little ginger-haired boy pointed his finger towards him. All the children put their hands out asking for money.
"Get away ye scabby little fuckers," roared Michael. Sean was delighted to hear his helpful voice and quickly pushed his way through the crowd of children as they pulled his coat. Sean and Michael made their way back to the van.
"Well, did you find out what you needed to know from Mamma Bella?"

"Kind of, she wasn't able to answer all my questions. What she was able to provide was definitely useful."

"So, back to base then."

"Yes, please,"

Michael could see Sean was distracted and kept quiet most of the journey back. Sean glanced at his watch anxious it was nearly four o'clock and he was to meet Alex in an hour. He requested to be left off somewhere close to the bus route. It would be easier to get back into the city if he left him off in the middle of Ballymun.
Sean kept twenty euros in his pocket to give to Michael, so as he pulled over at the side of the road, Sean handed it to him, thanked him and exited the car. Michael quickly added it to his winnings from the fight.

"Cheers boy, good luck!"

Sean knew he needed all the luck he could get to save his son's soul.

Traffic was bad and there was no sign of a bus or taxi and Sean took the opportunity to call his father. Sean found a quiet area to talk so no one could hear what would be deemed, an unusual conversation.

"Hello, how are you? I'm fine, progressing well, I think. What's your Granddad up to? Oh really! Yes, I believe I have found what we need. I just need to decipher it. No Kevin, you have to stay there to be safe. No, your Granddad is not crazy, I trust him to keep you safe until I can figure this out. No Kevin. No. No. Kevin! It's just for two or three days, you can handle that, can't you? Good. Put your Granddad on the phone, please…Dad? No, I didn't find the curse. I think I found the key though, the get-out clause to the curse. What do you mean how do I know? I visited the Travellers, yes, gypsies. I was told what I had was the part that comes after the curse, to allow the cursed souls to be saved. I came across it in an old diary, just by chance. No, I don't understand it yet. I have a student helping me later. Yes, she is a woman. I'm here to save my son Dad, nothing else. As soon as we figure it out, I'll be in touch again. Probably be later this evening. Ok, yes, I'll talk to you then. I have to go, there's a taxi coming. And Dad, go easy on the drink. You need your wits about you. Talk soon, bye."

Sean held out his hand to catch a taxi. He asked to be taken to the city centre. If this was a quick enough journey, he may have time to change before meeting Alex. He was hoping she would be as hungry as he was so they could chat and eat. They arrived at his hotel within twenty minutes and he quickly dashed to his room to change. For some reason, he was feeling a little nervous.

Chapter 6

"Yep, bye son. Keep me posted. Good luck," Brendan hung up. He was slightly relieved Sean was doing well with his research, but he was concerned for his grandson's mental health. He was not any good at dealing with children, especially teenagers, and had never built a relationship with any of his grandchildren, so assumed it must be difficult for Kevin to rely on him and trust him.

"Well, your Dad is doing well. He has someone helping him now, to figure out how to get rid of this curse. You'll be home before you know it," Brendan said confidently even with the doubts he had.

"Do you think so?" asked Kevin innocently.

"I don't understand what's going on. Why do I have to stay here? I know you said it's for my protection, but from what?"

Brendan rolled his eyes.

Had Kevin not remembered his recent nightmarish experience, had he not remembered screaming and telling them what, or who, he had seen?
"It's all in the stories I've been telling ye since ye were a little 'un. The Banshee wants revenge, she cursed the bloodline of our ancestors and since we, me and your Dad, married Irish girls, the cursed bloodline has become strong enough for the Banshee to return from the dark side. You need to stay here 'cause she can't come onto holy ground, it's your only protection. Do ye understand?"
"I think so Granddad," Kevin was still confused. Brendan knew Kevin had no idea how much danger he was in.
"Do ye want another cup of tea?" he asked.
"Yes please, Granddad, two sugars,"

Kevin watched the frail man leave the room and wondered if he was taking too much medication. He glanced all around the cramped room and up at the low ceiling. How would he cope being stuck here with some priest? While opening the drawers of the desk to put some clothes in he found a Bible.
"Great, all there is here is the Bible,"

Kevin shrugged his shoulders and thought of the magazines he hid under his mattress at home. He would just visualise the pictures if need be. Wait, how could he do such an act in the 'House of God'? He needed to control any urges, asleep or not.

It was only recently he was nearly exposed by his mother. He assumed she was asleep in bed yet she must have heard the noise coming from his room. He freaked as the door opened. Not wanting to be found in such a predicament he bellowed out false snores from beneath the covers. She whispered his name but he dared not answer. He had been more vigilant since then.

Brendan returned with a steaming cup and side plate in his hands, "Here boy, I made ye a sandwich. Father David only has ham or marmite in the fridge, so of course I chose ham,"
"Thanks, Granddad," not realizing he was so hungry until he smelled the fresh bread, which made his mouth water a little, Kevin devoured the sandwich.

There was now an awkward silence between them. Nothing was there to distract them from talking. No television, no video games, and no other grandchildren playing.
"How about I tell ye a story, would you like that? Keep your mind off everything…even for a few minutes," said his grandfather.
"Not about the Banshee I hope,"
"Nah, a story of circumstances. No scary story, just life. My life," Brendan began his story.

It started in Dublin city in the forties.

Brendan's father was an alcoholic who downed a bottle of whiskey a day. The only interaction he had with his children was with a belt and buckle on their behinds. It didn't matter whether they badly behaved or not, he never needed an excuse. He had eleven siblings in total, Brendan was third from the youngest, and they lived in a small three-bedroom house just outside the centre of the city. He shared his bed with three brothers and his room with four more. His sisters shared the other smaller bedroom. There would have been three more of them sharing except they had died from illnesses when they were quite young. They didn't have much, only a few wooden toys and a handful of books. All their clothes were hand-me-downs from grown-up cousins, except on Christmas Day. Their mother would always insist on taking their father's bonus from work and spend it on much needed clothes or material. It would be shameful to attend Christmas Day Mass in old clothes. What would the neighbours think?
Brendan was a boxer as a child and had won many fights. His photo had appeared in the national paper when he was only ten. The photographer was lucky to capture a fast fist going into the face of his unfortunate opponent. Brendan told this part with pride.

Kevin sat in awe of his grandfather's story.
"How many fights did you win Granddad?"

"Only eight, but I should have won many more and maybe even become a professional,"

"How Granddad?" One summer, while out gallivanting with his brothers, they'd sat on a bridge wall swinging their feet and ate fruit stolen from a local orchard. Brendan mocked one of his brothers who had bitten a caterpillar in half, hidden inside an apple. The mockery angered his brother so much he pushed Brendan off the ten-foot high bridge. They scarpered and left him lying there unconscious and bleeding. He awoke many hours later in the dark and struggled home with a sore head and blurred vision. Later, his brothers took the worst beating they'd ever experienced. His promising career as a boxer ended with one mistake. Although he was still able to throw a solid punch, his performance was now slower and he was unable to move and defend himself like he used to. It was the only activity he did to made his father proud.

"Aw, that's terrible, Granddad. Your brothers deserved a beating, they ruined your future."
"That's life, my boy, that's life,"

A few years later their father was offered a better paid job in London and they moved with five children in tow as the remainder had grown up and had families of their own. Brendan didn't return to school, instead he searched for work.

It was common in those days to leave school at a younger age to help support your family. His first job was to deliver milk to his neighbourhood every morning. He also worked as a hospital porter moving patients around. The doctors were rude and treated them badly so he didn't stay. He then settled in a factory making glass, even making the bottles he once delivered filled with milk, and stayed there for over forty years before he retired.

In the meantime, he met his lovely wife Deirdre, whose family had moved from Dublin to Liverpool. She was on a weekend excursion to London and they met in a little dingy nightclub. It was love at first sight for him and he travelled to Liverpool on his motorcycle every second week when his work shifts allowed it whereas she visited London only once a month. While on one of his visits he heard word of a man who was also seeking Deirdre's affection. Jealousy flooded within him and with one fist to the face the man fell to the ground and did not dare pursue Deirdre again.

Kevin giggled at the thought of his grandfather fighting over a girl.
"Find that funny do ye? When you fall in love, son, you would do the exact same,"
It was on one of her trips down, she told him she was two months' pregnant.

Without hesitation, he proposed and within two weeks they were married in his local church so as to not have a child out of wedlock.

"In them days it was the only option. If the girl wasn't married, the child would be a bastard and families would be gossiped about for years. So, we wed," Brendan took his flask out of his pocket and took a sip. He offered some to Kevin knowing he was too young, although the circumstances allowed for it this time. Kevin happily accepted the offer and took a large mouthful. The whiskey burned his throat, making him cough, and an inner heat rushed to his face. His cheeks burned up and he felt slightly light headed.

"Wow, strong stuff Granddad, thanks,"
"Well, I think you need it," Kevin nodded and listened as Brendan continued his story.

After that, they had their first child, a girl. They called her Catriona. Unfortunately, she died just two months later. The doctors said it was meningitis. Deirdre never recovered after losing her little one and, up until the day she died, she visited her tiny grave every year.
"I didn't know Granddad, I'm sorry,"
"Not even your Dad knows. No one does. It helped to have more children to keep her busy,"

Brendan's story didn't last too much longer. He said, "Once you have kids, that's it, life over. Even when they grow up, leave the house, get married, have kids, you're still a full-time parent," He thought they would finally have some peace in the house. Then Deirdre found a lump. There was no way out now. The worst scenario had happened and all the medicine in the world could not save her. He described how he felt when they were told the news. It started as a piercing pain in his heart and disbelief. Then he was angry and regretful, he wanted to do so much more with his wife. When she was gone, he felt empty and full of despair. It was all so final. Brendan repeated the word again, 'final', and wiped a little tear from the corner of his eye.
"Thanks for the story Granddad, it kept my mind busy,"

Kevin glanced out of the window and noticed it was getting dark. He was anxious, it would soon be time when his body would want to switch off and regenerate for the next day. His breathing quickened.
"Put your head between your knees and take deep breaths. You will be safe here, she can't get to you on holy ground,"
"You can't stop my dreams and I can't escape them." replied Kevin.

Chapter 7

Sean arrived at the meeting point just in time. As he glanced at his watch he heard a familiar voice calling his name. Alex waved through the crowd.
"Hi, I'm starving, are you? Where can we eat around here? Do you know of anywhere nice?" Alex giggled as she didn't even get a chance to say hello or to answer any of his questions. "What's so funny?" asked Sean.
"Let me answer at least one question before you move onto the next two or three please. Yes, I am hungry. We're beside Temple Bar which is full of bars and restaurants. Do you want a big portion of grub and somewhere we can talk?" asked Alex.
"That'll do nicely."

She brought him to a little bar on a street corner, dark and dirty but empty and peaceful.

They walked past plenty of venues, however the noise coming out of each one, from the music and customers, was deafening. Alex picked a quiet booth in the corner with dark blue upholstery worn down so much that the seams were frayed. The table was full of etchings of names, and 'waz ere'. Sean read the triangular-shaped menu on the table and instantly knew what he wanted... lasagne with garlic bread and a side salad. It sounded tantalizing. Alex ordered the same.
"So, what did you get up to today then? Did you do any sightseeing?"
"Well, I saw a library, a Traveller site, a bare-knuckle boxing match and had my fortune told,"
Alex found his list comical and laughed.
"Why are you in Ireland again?" she asked.
To Alex, this conversation was getting more interesting by the minute.
"I'm here to do some research on Irish mythology," Sean replied, he was unable lie to anyone so held his head low.
"Why do I get the feeling you are not telling me the truth. I mean, what has bare knuckle fighting got to do with mythology?" she asked.
"If I told you the truth, you wouldn't believe me,"
"Try me. You never know, I might believe you. Most Irish people know their own myths and legends you know. We learn it in school. Like the Children of Lir, Fionn MacCumhaill and the Pookha. All of these are Irish stories. So, tell me yours,"

"Okay. Ever heard of the Banshee?" asked Sean. Alex's eyes widened with curiosity. She did not expect to hear the name of one of the most well-known stories in Irish history.

"Who hasn't? There are many stories of the Banshee from different places and times. Some are of an old woman combing her hair, some are of a young beautiful fairy-like creature. It was said she haunts a few particular families in Ireland, but I don't ever remember being told why. The Scottish, Welsh and British all have their own versions too."

"So, there is no origin to any of these stories, no explanation as to why she is?" said Sean.

"No, not that I know of but these are only stories, you know that, don't you? I mean, you can't be over here just to research one old Irish myth. You could easily have found out all you need to know on the internet. So now is the time to be honest. If you want me to help, I want the truth."

Sean took a deep breath and started his chronicle with the death of a young gypsy girl, why he was there in person, what he needed from the Travellers and how his 'research' played a vital role in finding answers. Alex listened in disbelief nodding occasionally.

"If you want to leave now, I understand," said Sean.

"I'm not entirely convinced of your story as you can understand, but I would be interested in seeing how this all plays out. I'm not saying I don't believe in the afterlife either. I have a story of my own. I believe I saw a ghost once, well, we thought it was a ghost. I was in the Powerscourt Centre shopping with a friend. Powerscourt was the townhouse of a famous noble family. Anyway, we were walking out of a shop when we saw a young girl sitting in a wooden wheelchair. Her clothes and hair stood out even more. She had long dark blonde ringlets and the style of her dress was brownish with a decoration of frills, like a person from the 1800s. The experience gave me a terrible fright, my hands trembled and my heart fluttered. The worst of it was, she kept staring at us and it was as if no one else saw her. Apart from whispering 'Do you see her too?' we did not say a word until we passed her, and then quickly shuffled our way through the crowds until we were outside. This totally freaked us out and I didn't go back there for years. I know what I saw was real, so you can count me in,"

Sean smiled at Alex. The food arrived and not much more was said during the next twenty minutes as Sean devoured the full meal. He probably would have licked the plate only it was not the place or the company.
"Okay, what do you need me to translate?"

He handed her the photocopies of the transcripts and waited patiently as she skimmed through page after page. Alex was about three-quarters of the way through when she lifted her head and stared at Sean.

"I think I've found something. It was much easier since you told me the truth. I would have missed this had you not told me the full story. It doesn't mention the Banshee, probably because they didn't know what it was at the time, but it does mention a family of four being murdered by an evil spirit. The church had been their home for quite some time, two brothers had been brought up there by their parents, and they paid their way by working the land. Then it tells the story of the evening they didn't return from the fields, the priest sauntered outside to see why they had not returned before dark as they had done for sixteen years. He was met with a harrowing sight. The father, his wife and their two sons had been brutally slain. The men had been sliced into pieces with a scythe. The wife was alive, just barely. She told the priest she had tried to stop it from killing her sons, but then passed away. She had been inflicted with just one fatal injury, not a massacre like the men. They left behind one little girl, who was now in the custody of the church until she reached an age when she was able to leave and married a local boy from the village. They had children of their own," Alex paused.

"That's not really helpful," said Sean.

"Ah, I am not finished yet, you need to have patience my dear. I was just taking a breather. It then says she gave birth to a baby boy after three girls. So she returned to the church when he was a young boy, begging them to take him in. She told the priest of the curse on her family, her son was in danger and needed to be saved. They thought she was insane and secluded her from everyone. With her uncontrollable behaviour, they threw her into a madhouse run by the Sisters of Mercy. While incarcerated, it's recorded she kept repeating these words over and over again until her death, 'the noble mount, the wailing wall'. It does not say what happened to her son."

Sean reached for the scrap of paper from his inside jacket pocket and jotted down what Alex had just said, "I read through an old diary earlier today in the library and I found a quote with similar wording. There was nothing about a wailing wall, but I'm guessing this is related," He showed Alex the paper and she agreed they had a connection, "I asked the gypsy woman about this and she didn't know what it meant. Do you know?" asked Sean.

"No, I'm sorry, I don't. But I know someone who might. He works in Trinity College. His name is Stephen."
Alex took her phone outside, for some privacy, and dialled the college requesting to speak to Dr. McWilliams.

After two minutes of being kept on hold, Alex was put through to Stephen and asked him for his help.

"I'm calling in that favour you owe me," she read out the passage and gave a bit more detail surrounding the research, then paused awaiting a response. Alex jotted some details down on the same scrap of paper, said where they were and hung up.

Alex and Stephen had a complicated history. They had known each other for a long time as they ran in similar social circles, although with Stephen being a few years older than Alex he did not show much interest to begin with. It was only when Alex started dating a friend of Stephen, then he grew a curiosity towards her, specifically when he heard how great she was. He did not want to betray a friend so waited patiently. It started with a wink and a smile. Stephen wanted Alex to know he was keen. Their social activities involved many weekend house parties hosted by students in rented accommodation. Free to do whatever.

It all went a little sour at a graduation party both Stephen and Alex were invited to. Alex was now single and sure enough Stephen was on the prowl. Women practically threw themselves at his disposal, even knowing his reputation, to experience a night of passion only to be discarded when used.

Alex on the other hand was strong minded enough not to easily fall for sweet whispers. She liked him, what was not to like? He was charismatic, funny, intelligent and witty. All the attributes a woman would want in a man except he was missing the most important one . . . fidelity.

In the large residence, the partygoers had dispersed throughout the house and back garden. Those downstairs danced and mingled whereas upstairs a lot more was happening. Stephen grabbed Alex by the hand and pulled her up the stairs for some quiet time.

The first room stunned Stephen and Alex, not by the goings-on, instead by the number involved in the debauchery. Seven or eight people were on the queen-sized bed all entangled with each other. Heat, sweat and the smell of sex seeped out of the room. Others just sat watching the display, aroused yet controlling their urges. Men groaned in gratification and woman hollered with excitement.

Stephen closed the door and they scampered off giggling like little schoolchildren. Another room, filled with smoke from an abundance of bongs, contained the 'stoners'. They found a corner office empty, mostly because it was cold and dull with only one chair. Stephen took out a small bag of cocaine and tipped some out onto the mahogany desk.

Refusing the offer, Alex was a little appalled he would use drugs. Reading her expression, Stephen excused himself saying he only did it once in a while. Sniffing one line he left the other for afterwards. They chatted for a time until he touched the nape of her neck and kissed her. Alex responded and panted as he moved his lips to her chest. Stephen pulled up her dress and slipped his hand into her panties, his other hand was making room to sit her on the desk. Alex knew his purpose yet was too aroused to stop, instead she unbuckled his belt and opened his trousers. He lifted Alex up onto the desk and bent down, opened her legs and embraced her.

Unknown to the enthusiastic couple, a raid was being conducted by the Garda National Drugs Unit as it was rumoured drug dealers would be visiting the party to supply the guests. Uniformed Gardai swooped through most of the rooms and ransacked all hiding places. They discovered scores of pills and bags of cocaine.

They burst into the office just as a semi-naked Alex was putting a condom on Stephen. She was quickly able to fix her dress, but Stephen had difficulty pulling up his trousers and fell over during the scuffle. They questioned the line of drugs on the table. Panicking, because of his career, Stephen denied any involvement and accused Alex of possessing the drugs.

Speechless, Alex could tell Stephen was terrified of being discovered as a drug user. If the college found out, he may lose his position. Even being anti-drugs Alex confessed to owning and using the cocaine.

They spent many hours in the Garda station pleading their innocence, insisting they were just simply there for the party. With no evidence against them and no previous record, the Gardai released them with a caution. Alex lost some respect for Stephen that night yet understood why he did it. Apologizing with flowers, chocolates and many invitations to dinner, Stephen eventually backed off when Alex ignored all his text messages. She was still attracted to him and liked him, but the trust was gone and it would never be the same between them.

Stephen knew he had a debt to pay and was willing to do anything to redeem himself.

"Stephen is intrigued and wants to come over. He said his experience and study, although ambiguous at times, has turned up similar verbiage before but not as detailed as this. I hope you don't mind me talking about this with someone else. Stephen has deep knowledge of the history in Ireland. He is in the Department of History so he should be helpful," said Alex.

"No, I don't mind, it can't hurt at this stage. If I don't find out where it is or what it means soon, my son will probably have to spend the rest of his life in a church." he replied.

"I still don't understand, why your son and not you?" asked Alex.
"Yep, I was waiting for this question. My father believes the bloodline with the curse has weakened for many generations due to mixing other blood to the cursed family line. She has always been there, stuck between heaven and hell. Waiting. Warning. Now it seems the cursed bloodlines have found each other and is making her entity stronger. My father married an Irish lass and so did I. It is now strong enough to haunt my son in his dreams. My father warned me this could happen. I didn't listen thinking he was just rambling. My son has had the same recurring nightmare for weeks. Again, I didn't listen. Kevin came to me for answers I didn't have or didn't want to have,"

"Your wife must be worried sick," Alex scrunched her face.
"Ex-wife, and she doesn't know anything about this. He's our only child so I didn't want her to have a breakdown,"

'I understand,"

Alex stopped being inquisitive. He told Alex where Kevin was now and his father was taking care of him. Alex interrupted their conversation by waving her hand towards the front of the bar. Dr. McWilliams had arrived.

A tall man, quite slender with thinning black hair slicked back to the neck, strode over confidently. He wore black jeans and matching shirt with pointy cowboy style boots. He reminded Sean of an ageing rock star that couldn't accept time was taking its toll on his riveting youth. Sean had expected him to be much older, being a doctor in the top college of Ireland, but guessed his age to be around forty. Instantly he held out his hand to greet Sean. Sean received the gesture with a smile and invited Dr. McWilliams to sit down and join them. Sean noticed how Stephen glared at Alex, he undoubtedly thought more of her than just a student.

"Please, call me Stephen," he requested.

"So, I hear you're in Ireland following some breadcrumbs and from what Alex told me, you're having difficulties solving the riddles to where a certain location is. I've seen similarities of this 'fable' a couple of times over the years, but due to the Chinese whisper pattern of generations, the wording has diminished or changed slightly. So let me see what you've found,"

Alex handed him the scrap of paper she was holding and they waited patiently while Stephen read the extract. He started to grin, which turned into a big smile.

"This sums it up for me. When I saw similar quotations, here and there, over the years, it was missing the key words you have here. I had always thought this tale was discussing our precious and ancient Newgrange, older than the pyramids of Egypt and Stonehenge you know, as this has a heavily decorated 'wall', well a boulder is probably a better word. Then there are the other two mounds nearby, Knowth and Dowth. These all have noteworthy walls and stones, basin stones to be exact, this parable could be referencing. There is also Brian Boru's Fort, he was one of our famous High Kings of Ireland and is located in County Clare, but I believe this is long after Brian's rule. Then when I saw what you two had discovered here, all the pieces came together. It has to be describing the Hill of Tara. Where on earth did you find this?"

"One from a diary of a woman many years ago and the other from the manuscript of a religious order,"

"Fascinating. I never thought of researching diaries," Stephen was angry with himself and slapped his leg. Alex sat back in relief and assurance, she had definitely made the right decision in contacting Stephen.

Sean recognised the name of the place. He recalled reading an article in the paper a few years back about a protest to save the area from a motorway being built over the site. Some celebrities turned up to show their support, they objected and luckily it worked.
Stephen explained more, "On the Hill of Tara is a stone, called *Lia Fáil*, it's Irish for '*Stone of Destiny*', where the High Kings of Ireland were crowned. According to legend, if a series of challenges were met by the would-be king, the stone would wail when he touched it. The new King would then be crowned. The Hill of Tara is the noble mount and the Stone of Destiny is the Wailing Wall. I just don't understand the 'innocence' part,"

"I may be able to help," said Sean.
Stephen sat and listened to Sean as he told the story of the Banshee and the curse on his bloodline for many generations, "Are you serious?" he asked Sean, then turned towards Alex, "Tell me this guy is not for real?"
"He is Stephen. I'm cynical of this story too, but I believe Sean is genuine and honest with us. He fears for his son's life and that is evidently real. Even if you don't regard it as the truth, as a friend, I'm asking you to go along with this for now,"
"I don't care if you think I'm crazy. I'm not here for your acceptance, I just needed help working this out and you've done that, so thank you. I think I know what I have to do," added Sean abruptly.

He then held Alex's hand, making Stephen squirm in his seat.

"Alex, you don't have to help me any further. I really appreciate the time and effort you have given me, but I would understand if you want to forget all about this and go home,"

"No chance, you're not getting rid of me. I told you, I want to see how this plays out," replied Alex.

"All right, maybe I was a little hasty. I'll assist you anyway I can but I'm going to need some more details on when this curse started. I'll tell you why in a little while," said Stephen.

Stephen had strong feelings for Alex and did not want to miss an opportunity to be involved if she was. Sean's instincts told him Stephen's affections were not fully requited; he even sensed a little tension. Sean sat back in the chair, rubbing the ever growing stubble on his chin, and thought logically about how far back in time this story could have originated. He remembered Elizabeth's journal said over five generations and that was in the 1850s. Life expectancy for the lower class in those days was probably around forty. So, working it out, he calculated it most likely would have happened around 1650, taking into consideration that life expectancy of the men was much shorter than women.

"Possibly around 1650, give or take a few decades. I think that's the closest I can guess to when this happened."

"Then this search has become a little harder because during the rebellion of 1798, Irishmen formed a camp on the hill and were attacked and defeated by the British army. The Stone of Destiny was moved in remembrance of the 400 rebels who died on the hill that day. So we need to find out where the Stone was before it was moved,"

Sean sighed, realising there always had to be a catch. "Don't worry, I'm sure this is documented and the original location will be shown on some old map filed away somewhere. I'll check the archives tomorrow to see what I can find," said Stephen.

"Great. By the way, where is the Hill of Tara?" asked Sean.

"You're in luck, my friend, it's in County Meath, just north of Dublin, so not too far away," replied Stephen.

"What do you intend to do?"

"I may not have understood where to find the site, but I understand the next part. If there are any remains, they need to be moved to sacred ground,"

Alex and Stephen were astonished.

"Don't be so shocked, it is what I must do to save my son's life. I'm sure you would do the same if you were in my shoes. So, we should meet tomorrow night, if you're still willing to help me. I think it is best to start our journey in the early hours to avoid detection but also to ensure we are nearer daylight time... as a precaution,"

Stephen speculated as to why they would need to be there so early.

"It would not be greatly received if you openly dig on a heritage site without permission," Stephen remarked.

"I have no choice. I'll do a little research on where the stone was before," Sean knew he would never be given permission.

"And given you may not determine the exact location of the remains, how do you expect to find them?"

"I'll have to dig a lot of holes,"

"Well, I may be able to help you there too. I have a friend working in the National History Museum who can provide us with a ground-penetrating radar. This apparatus takes an image, using sound waves, of what's underground so you can see bones or whatever else solid might be there,"

"That's so good of you, thank you, I really appreciate it,"

"Stephen, you're brilliant. I knew out of everyone you'd be the one able to help Sean," said Alex.

Alex suggested they have a few drinks to relieve the stress of the day, to get a taste of Irish culture and to discuss the plan for tomorrow night. Sean was hesitant, it was not part of his plan to socialise while he was here. Nevertheless, he reckoned it was better than waiting and staring at the four walls of his hotel room.

"I just need to ring my father and give him an update. He'll be wondering what's happening. I'll go back to my hotel room to ring, if you don't mind,"
Stephen had to complete an evening lecture and made his way back to the college. Alex wanted to change out of her clothes. She didn't want to waste time or effort going home and then travel back into the city. Sean offered her his hotel room.
Stephen was disappointed, he had hoped Alex would ask to go with him. As they left the bar they walked their separate ways yet Stephen continuously peeked back to watch for any body language. He wished she would agree to go to a hotel room with him in the future.

Sean struggled to open his hotel door. He slid the card into the slot but the red light appeared over and over again. Alex suggested he pull the card out a little slower, he did and thankfully the light turned green. She didn't comment on the room as magnolia was not her favourite colour but at least it was clean. Sean quickly rummaged through his bag and selected some suitable attire, he had not expected a night out while he was here. He brought them into the bathroom to change. It was the only other room available. Alex gestured she would be making a call and sat at the desk. Sean could overhear the conversation quite clearly while he stripped. Alex was talking to her mother explaining she wouldn't be home until tonight.

She lied and said she had to stay to study for an exam and needed access to books belonging to students in her class. Her voice raised its tone with anger. She was unable to mind her nephews this evening and ordered her sister to take responsibility and mind her own children. The goodbye was quite abrupt and Alex sighed with anguish when she hung up. Sean felt it was safe to come out.

"All ok?"

"Yes, fine, thank you, just family issues as usual. I spent my teenage years bringing up my younger brothers and sisters, now they expect me to mind their kids too. I could do with a distraction and now I have one,"

"As they say, you can choose your friends, but can't choose your family," Sean said supportively.

Alex nodded and headed towards the bathroom with a small backpack. Sean was curious how she could fit a change of clothes in such a compact bag. Three minutes later, Alex emerged wearing clothes like she was about to enter a triathlon. Sean liked how the Lycra clung to her shapely hips and thighs. Her pumps took three inches off her height and now had to bend her neck to talk with Sean. It was time Sean phoned Brendan. Alex offered to wait downstairs in the lobby and left.

"Hi, it's me. How is Kevin doing? Good. Yes, Dad, I was able to work out from the passages where I need to go and what I need to do, with a little help of course. Who? Oh, the student I told you about earlier and a Trinity College doctor. I believe her remains are buried at the Hill of Tara in County Meath. The only issue is just finding the exact location. The doctor, Stephen, will be checking this for me tomorrow. He needs to find some old aerial maps. I need to dig up the remains and move them to holy ground. Well, I hope that's what I have to do. I know, I need more than hope, but I'm out on a whim here Dad and it's the most logical solution. 'Sacred terrain' Dad, remember? It means sacred ground; this will end the tale. No, I won't risk doing it in the evening. I want to do it closer to sunrise, it will be safer. She is only heard or seen at night. What do you mean, what will I be doing tomorrow day? I am going to check out the area, see if it is all accessible and then locate the nearest sacred ground. Yes, I will keep you up to date. I'm going to rest now, do a bit more research and then go to sleep."

Sean didn't want his father to know he was going out for drinks probably because he would think it was inappropriate. Sean felt the same and would not have enjoyed his own company for the night. Going out would help keep his sanity and having a few drinks meant he could sleep heavily and not have a night of tossing and turning.

"Goodnight Dad, please tell Kevin he'll be okay. I'll ring you again tomorrow evening when I'm planning the excavation. Okay, talk tomorrow. Goodbye."

Sean saw a coffee shop and yearned for some strong caffeine to keep him awake and energised for the evening ahead, "Would you like a coffee?" asked Sean.
"No thanks."

She checked her watch four times while awkwardly waiting outside as Sean queued and stomped her feet to keep moving. The temperature had dropped significantly. The customer in front of him was an obvious drug taker with dirty clothes, rotten teeth… a dishevelled sight.

"Can I get a tea and a KitKat junkie, I mean chunky, a KitKat chunky?" he asked.

Sean had never heard this harsh Dublin accent before, yet he understood the error made and the irony in it. He sniggered then coughed to hide it. The man turned knowing what sound had been made first.
"Have ye got a problem bud?"
"No, I just want to order a cappuccino. Can I pay for yours too?" Sean asked.

He hoped this would defuse a situation from escalating.

He agreed and continued to call him 'bud' as he thanked him again and again and left the shop. Sean just smiled, delighted there would be no trouble. This was not his first experience with a junkie. One had tried to steal from him in London last year. He had just taken money from an ATM and was approached from behind with the threat to 'hand over his cash or else'. He did not see a weapon or a needle in their hands so confronted his attacker by throwing the copy books he carried onto the ground and challenged him. Surprised by his contender the thief shrugged his shoulders and casually walked away. It was a stupid act of bravery, fortunately luck was in his favour.

Sean stood beside Alex sipping from the little hole in the lid and kept the cup near to his chin to let the steam warm his face.

Alex opted for a famous tourist bar, The Auld Dubliner, so Sean could understand a typical night out in Dublin. She beckoned Sean to follow her through the busy streets of Temple Bar. People were everywhere, some stood in groups, mostly teenagers, mucking about having fun. The rest were on their way home from work or going in and out of bars, intoxicated and finding it difficult to walk on the cobblestones that flowed through the streets like a dirty river filled with waste and moving carcasses.

They approached the chosen bar and Sean considered it stereotypical of an Irish drinking hole. Traditional Irish music radiated through the doors when they swung open with every customer who came and left. What was wrong with him discovering his traditional roots while he was here, he thought. He did not expect to enjoy the evening, yet now he had the excuse to find out what his father had been talking about for most of his life, having visited family many times over the years. His father, although in London, socialised with his Irish friends in Irish pubs all his life.

His first impressions were not good. The smell of stale ale and stout was unpleasant. As a child, his father came home with a particular odour many times. He did not like it then either.

"What would you like to drink?" asked Alex.
"No, please let me get these. What would you like?"
"Ok, but I'll get the next round. I'll have a pear cider please; any brand will do,"

Sean ordered himself a beer and brought them to the table where Alex had sat down. Small grubby stools filled the floor with worn floral designs. There was limited room to sit and Sean's knees kept brushing the backside of a woman in a group beside them. He repeatedly said sorry every few minutes.

The musician was upstairs so the noise was not too overbearing. He stared at the pint in front of him and awaited that feeling of the first mouthful. It was smooth, cold and crisp and these qualities encouraged him to take another straight after.

"Hey, slow down there. The beer over here is stronger, you need to set a pace and stick to it. So, tell me a bit about you Sean. For a person I'm about to break some law with, I don't know much about you,"

"I'll tell you if you go next. Well, to start with, I'm a history teacher in a secondary school for boys in London. Before you say a word, I'm not trained in Irish history although I do know about the plantations, the famine and, of course, the 1916 Rebellion. The state of affairs that affected the British. I'm on special leave at the moment because I confronted, they say assaulted, a student who threatened my son Kevin. I just grabbed the little punk by his clothes and told him to back off. I was disciplined. I met my wife, Claire, when I was a young man and we wed soon after. We fell out of love and have been divorced for a few years now. I moved back in with my father to save money and help him a little. He's getting on in years now and we are all, my siblings and I, concerned for his wellbeing since my mother passed away. As I was the only single one, they nominated me for the job.

And lastly, I hope to go travelling across Asia within the next year or two, to teach English until I save enough money to make my way back home,"

"Well, you were honest, so I guess I'll have to be too. I'm a Dublin girl, from a place called Crumlin. I was an honours student but left school and hung around with a bad crowd. When I wasn't taking care of my brothers and sisters while my parents drank the local pub dry, I was hanging around fields getting drunk or high. I came to my senses when my best friend fell into the local canal and drowned. We were all too high to save her. It was a shock to the system and I was devastated. I regret it all now and have my life back on track. I worked two jobs to keep me on the straight and narrow. My colleagues saw potential and encouraged me to go back to school and finish my exams. I then decided to go to college as a mature student, the two jobs paid for my entrance fee. My part-time jobs now pay for my yearly fees. I always loved the Irish language so selected the course I'm doing now. I'm currently single, living with my mother, with no intentions of settling down until I have the career I want,"

Sean found Alex endearing, he listened to every single word she said. He watched her and noticed she licked her lips after each sip from her glass.

Alex turned her glare towards the door, Stephen had just entered and was making his way through the crowds towards their table, "Finished so soon?" she asked.
"Yes, I let my class go home early. They were a little surprised, but I gave them a few extra tasks to do for the next night. So, can I get you all a drink?"

At the bar, it didn't take Stephen long to charm a petite strawberry blonde. He moved closer and whispered in her ear. She flirted with him, gently touched his arm as her head bent back in laughter. He returned to the table and slipped a bit of paper in his front pocket, tapping his conquest with a winning smile. Sean was never good at talking to the ladies. He lacked charm and confidence. All he had was his sense of humour and baby blue eyes, so his wife told him. Alex did not seem impressed by the antics of Stephen.

As it was nearing the end of the evening, with plenty of drinks consumed, Stephen broke up the chit-chat conversation and asked the ominous question they all dreaded to discuss.
"So, what are the plans for tomorrow?"

"I will go out to The Hill of Tara tomorrow morning. I want to check out the mounds and the surrounding area. I need to ensure there is holy ground nearby and also I need to be sure we won't get disturbed. I'll need to hire a car and buy some equipment. Stephen, you will get the details we need with the location of where the Stone of Destiny used to be and also the radar machine. Are you okay transporting it?"

"Yes, it's not too big. Probably the size of a large pram so it should fit in the back of my car,"

"Cheers Stephen but I don't want either of you getting into trouble for the actions I have to take. I'll be doing all the illegal activities," Sean said.

Alex interrupted, "Hold on. We'll still be considered co-conspirator, but you only live once, right? You can go in my car tomorrow and I'm coming with you,"

"What about your college and work? I can't ask you to drop what you're doing for me,"

"It's only one day. Don't fret, I'll make up for it,"

"Thank you, Alex,"

As Sean talked through the rest of the plan, he spotted a cloaked figure in the corner of the room facing him.

The grey cloak covered the entire body with complete darkness under a large hood. It stood motionless. Sean paused and stood up. His heart pounded in his chest with fear and rage. Blood rushed to his face and adrenaline pumped through his veins.

Alex and Stephen were stunned as Sean darted towards the other side of the room. People crossed his path and he moved them out of his way which was followed by grunts from the unforgiving patrons. He drew nearer and reached out to grab the cloak. In an instance, a party of young women dressed in pink and black, with penis-shaped accessories, blocked his path. When he squeezed through the human traffic the figure had disappeared. Sean gasped in air to regain his breath. A bewildered audience had gathered, all staring in silence. He sheepishly waded back towards the table, bending his head low and making apologetic excuses to all.

"What was that all about?" asked Stephen.

"It was her. She must know what I am here to do," their bewildered expressions told Sean they did not know what he said, "The Banshee. She was over there watching me,"

"Now I know you're crazy," laughed Stephen arrogantly.

"I don't care what you think. I need to be careful, she is getting stronger each day," he snarled.
"Hey boys, now, now, let's keep it cool. No need to get hot headed. Stephen, if you don't like it, don't help. It's gonna be a long day tomorrow, so let's all go and get some rest," said Alex.

Stephen did not utter another opposing word and agreed to meet them at three o'clock the following morning on Westmoreland Street. Sean was glad Alex kept the peace. He didn't appreciate Stephen's attitude and may have lashed out at him physically if not for her. It was nearly midnight and the three of them stood outside and said goodbye.

Alex confirmed she would collect Sean in the morning to view the Hill of Tara. They had a plan and tomorrow's tasks were imperative to it being successful.

Chapter 8

Kevin stared at the ceiling for a long time. He shuffled in the uncomfortable bed and felt every spring protruding into his back. How had he ended up in such a place? He wasn't any way religious so how could being here save him? A knock on the door echoed throughout the room. It was Father David.

"Come in,"

"Hi Kevin! I'm checking you're okay before I retire to bed. I have an early start in the morning helping the homeless so I need my sleep."

Kevin saw Father David more closely now. He was not as old as he had originally thought. He was quite athletic and only a few wrinkles around the eyes.

Kevin guessed him to be in his late thirties, the beard made him appear older. Guitars hung from the sitting room wall, one with the name 'Dave 'The Snake' Sabo' scribbled on the front in black marker. Kevin had no idea who that was but assumed he was from some rock band from the 70s or 80s. Kevin wondered why this man had dedicated most of his existence to follow a life most logical people would consider absurd. Not being able to find love and have a family was unthinkable in this day and age.

"Father, I have a question? What makes people believe in something you can't see or feel? There is no proof God exists so how can he protect us?"
"Well, Kevin, we can only believe what we feel in our hearts. I believe there is a greater power that brings all the good into this world otherwise it would be brutal and ruthless. Let me explain it another way,

I once read 'Faith is like electricity. You can't see it, but you can see the light.' To me, the goodness in people is the light of God shining through. Once there is light in the world, there will always be someone willing to protect you. Your grandfather was a bit sketchy on the details. Do you want to tell me what's going on?"

"I don't want to discuss it yet. I'm still trying to get my head around it. I hope you don't mind."

Father David did not want to push Kevin into an answer so wished him a good night. He trusted Brendan and knew he was a good man. Brendan would not bring illegal trouble to the church. His room was opposite Kevin's and he was asleep within five minutes.

Kevin heard loud snoring and knew he was in for a restless night. He was exhausted, his eyes sore, his brain working overtime. He paced the room back and forth, each time he glanced out of the small square window, knowing she was leering at him from across the street; waiting.

Father David grasped Kevin by the shoulders and shook him, "Wake up, you're having a nightmare," Kevin jolted upwards nearly colliding heads with Father David. He stared blankly at the wall in front of him, then curled his body into the foetal position and whimpered. Father David tried to comfort him, but the whispers "She's going to get me." repeated out until the morning light.

Chapter 9

After a full Irish breakfast in the hotel, Sean waited on Westmoreland St for Alex to collect him. Traffic was back to back and Sean glanced at the drivers passing by so not to miss her. It was not long before Sean heard a large car horn repeating its annoying, boisterous sound. Alex drove an old little red Mini and parked in the bus lane. At first Sean thought it in good condition for a car made in '93. After further inspection of the frame, which was covered with rust, he hoped it was strong enough to carry two adults.

"C'mon then, hop in,"

The suspension was affected when he sat down and the creaking sounds didn't improve his assurance in the vehicle. They chatted briefly about the previous night, the weather and breakfast. Any topic related to Banshees or grave digging did not raise its ugly head.

Sean took in all the sights as Alex concentrated on directions. The Hill of Tara was quite a difficult place to find. They lost their way twice, but after an hour, they eventually arrived at their destination.

The morning sun shone brightly and the crisp air filled his lungs to the brim. It was quiet and Sean heard sheep bleating in the distance. The entrance was easy to access with a simple push gate and a low surrounding wall, completely unsecured. Alex complained about the sheep shit everywhere. It was unavoidable. Two small mounds were clearly visible as they tracked up the slope. They passed a smaller mound enclosed by railings, Sean glanced at the signage, and stepped backwards when his brain interpreted the relevance of the images and wording.

"Oh fuck. These mounds were excavated back in the 50s. What if they found the remains? My plan is ruined,"

"Wait, Sean. Don't start panicking yet, excavation happened on the mounds and surrounding areas. Remember what Stephen told us, the large stone was moved to that location after the slaughter of the United Irishmen in 1798, and you believe the murder happened before, so we won't be digging on the mound. We'll be digging further out. Hopefully Stephen will come up trumps with the information we need,"

"And the radar machine." Sean added.
They clambered up the hill. Alex reached the top much faster than Sean. He put that down to his age as he was around ten or twelve years older. Those few years really made a difference. Alex peeked back at Sean struggling to keep his balance on the slope and held out her hand to support him. As he clasped her petite hand, he felt how soft and delicate her skin was compared to his rough older skin. He did not want to let go.

Sean viewed the landscape and appreciated for the first time how picturesque Ireland and his surroundings were. He slowly turned full circle and appreciated the beautiful scenery surrounding him.

"I don't believe we'll have any problems later. There is no security. No one will be around to witness what we intend to do. It's surprising, but also a relief. The Church is not really Holy ground now it is a visitor's centre. However, the graveyard still is. It's still blessed ground. That's where I need to bury what remains of the gypsy girl."

They heard voices coming from the direction of the church. The first of today's sightseers had arrived. Loud Americans in their oversized bright coloured raincoats were taking pictures and spreading across the area like locusts consuming a cornfield. Within minutes Sean and Alex were encircled by tourists.

Sean, wanting to fit in, read the plaques sparsely located around the mounds. He did find it fascinating that these mounds were the place they crowned the High Kings of Ireland and assumed the mounds were the last resting place of those Kings hundreds and thousands of years ago, similar to the Egyptians using the pyramids to bury the great Pharaohs.

"Okay, I think it's time to go. I've seen enough," said Sean. They made their way out of the grounds and escaped the filling car park.

"What now?" asked Alex, "We have all day to burn time,"

"Well, I need to get a car big enough to carry the radar machine and other equipment, like a shovel, to help with the dig. Do you want to get some lunch first?"

Alex smiled and said she knew of the perfect place. Sean was feeling nervous. In less than twenty-four hours this would all be over. He thought of his son and wondered if he was doing right by his son, would he really be safe?

"When we stop, can you please ring Stephen to ask how he is getting on? Without him, I'm screwed,"

Chapter 10

"Hello... long time, no speak my friend. I'm fine, thanks. I have a favour to ask of you. I need to borrow the museum's ground-penetrating radar. Yes, I know it's a lot to ask. Eh, I'll need it today. Calm down, I'll bring it back tomorrow morning. No one will even know it's gone. Yes, I promise I'll take special care of it. No, I'm not going treasure hunting. Actually, I'd prefer not to say. Okay, okay... I'm helping someone find the remains of a body. No, no, no, don't worry. It's from a long, long time ago. Well, you know me, always trying to lend a helping hand. How did you know? Alex, her name's Alex. Yes, she's worth it to me. Right, I'll see you in a little while, I'll be there around five. Thanks Peter. Cheerio."

Stephen was on his lunch hour and thought it was the perfect time to search for old aerial maps while most of the students were not around.

It would have been drawn by hand, of a heritage site, nevertheless it was still a map, so he had to think, history or geography. After all his years in the history department, he never came across such a map so it had to be in the geography department.

In the Freeman Library, Stephen searched the catalogue for heritage maps with no luck. He would have to dig a little deeper. The librarian searched through the archive but the oldest they had, of County Meath, was from 1914. There were plenty of Dublin maps dating back to the 1800s but maps of other counties were limited. The librarian suggested asking the Head of the Department of Natural Sciences.

Stephen had now only thirty minutes to track down the head before lunchtime was over and lectures would carry on all afternoon. He checked the canteen and saw one of the Assistant Professors conversing with a student.

"Sorry to interrupt Dr. Curran, can you please tell me where I can find Professor Declan? I need to speak to him urgently."

"No need to sound so professional Stephen, it is lunchtime. You should find him in his office, he usually has lunch there."
Stephen made his way to the office and tapped gently on the door.

"It better be important if you are knocking at this time," was the response.

Stephen peeked in and apologised for disturbing him. From top to bottom on both sides, the interior was fitted out with cabinets. Professor Declan sat at a large mahogany desk and had a sandwich neatly placed on a starched white napkin. He stood up to greet Stephen. The pinstripe suit he wore had a creased line down the front of each leg and his comb-over strategically placed and divided out evenly over the small bald patch. Bottles of hand sanitiser were lined up his desk and not a speck of dust could be seen. Stephen quickly established he was a perfectionist and possibly suffered from an obsessive-compulsive disorder. He thought of how the Professor might react if he saw his unkempt messy workspace.

"Hi Declan. I hope you can help me please. I need what you have on the Hill of Tara, historically. I need to find the original location of Lia Fáil for a class I'm doing on Irish Heritage sites. There is no information in the history archives on the subject or in the geography rooms so I was advised to ask you,"

"Yes, yes, you've come to the right place, come in. Yes, yes, I have a number of maps of Meath in my personal collection. Let me have a gander,"

Stephen had not heard that expression since he was a child, when his Grandmother would search for some treats.

Professor Declan was quite a short man, he struggled to reach up to open a large drawer above him. Each county of Ireland was given its own drawer and alphabetically tagged.

Now standing on a stool, he flicked through multiple suspension files until he found a large plastic folder.

"Ah ha, yes, yes, here it is. Now you know I can't give this to you, but you can take a copy of it," Declan carefully spread out the maps on his desk. He studied each one until he reached the one he was searching for. "Yes, yes, this is it. I hope your hands are clean. I remember where this came from believe it or not, it was in someone's attic for a long time and ended up in a charity shop of all places. Yes, yes, I was out shopping to buy some books and found this treasure. Amazing!"

He delicately removed it from the pile and placed it on top. Stephen studied the hand drawn map and searched for the location of where the stone used to be. His finger moved through the list of monuments and finally he found it.

"Yes, yes, there it is," Professor Declan clapped his hands with excitement.
Stephen photocopied the map and brought it back to the office.

"Thanks Declan. This is a great help."
"Yes, yes, no problem. If I can help with anything else, just let me know."

Stephen wanted to ask him to stop saying 'yes, yes', it started to irk him and left immediately. His phone rang as he was about to return to class.

"Hi Alex! I'm getting on well, thanks. I have a copy of an old map with the original location and I'm collecting the radar in a while. What are the plans for this evening? Are we going out for drinks again? No! Okay, yes, I suppose it would be a bad idea if we are all meeting at 3am. Tell Sean he doesn't need to hire a car or van, I'll drive. My Audi should be big enough, but it might be a little squashed in the back if three of us are going in it. The radar should fit in the trunk, if you have other items, I suggest you put them in the back seat. Right, see you then. Yes, 3am. Westmoreland St. I won't be late. Bye."

Stephen felt disappointed and jealous. He knew Alex would be spending the remainder of the day with Sean; alone. He bit his lip and removed any thought of them together, sexually.

Throughout the remainder of his lectures, Stephen was unable to concentrate. He verbally fumbled his words as he thought of the illegal acts he would be committing later. Was one woman worth the lengths he was going to? He had resorted to many a misdemeanour in the past, yet never as crazy as this. After college, Stephen drove to the National Museum, where his name had been given to the security guard to let him through the employee gates. Peter was waiting outside with the radar. Stephen was relieved when he saw how compact it was. It would fit in the trunk.

"You owe me big time."

"I know, I know, I really appreciate it, Peter."

"Well, here it is. Please be extremely careful with this. It's an expensive piece of equipment. It can be used for day to day construction work or archaeology. Here, I'll show you how to use it."

Peter first demonstrated how to open out and fold the radar, the easy part. He then turned the screen on to show how the technology worked.

"The transmitter submits radio waves into the ground and any anomalies beneath the surface will be picked up by the antenna which sends a message to the receiver. Basically, the radio wave will bounce back if it hits a solid item and the screen here will show a little arch shape. Remember, it will pick up everything underground. Pipes, metal and, hopefully, the items you want...bones. Now I want to know a little more about what you are up to. Whose bones are they?"

"His mission is to find the remains of someone allegedly murdered hundreds of years ago. Yes, weird, I know. There should be no pipes there and we do know the location, so I'll only be screening a small area of the ground,"

"So, who is we? Not someone who'll steal my equipment I hope!"

"No, no, he's a teacher from the UK and a friend of Alex. Don't judge me like that. She is a beautiful woman inside and out. Hey, you would never have met your gorgeous wife if it wasn't for me,"

"You are not the monogamous type, Stephen, you only want her because you can't have her. If you started dating, it would not be long before you moved on to your next conquest. It's just who you are. Is Isabelle still stalking you?"

"Yes, four Facebook messages, twelve tweets and sixteen texts in one week,"

"You can't just love them and leave them these days you know, there are too many ways to contact people. We can't hide in the shadows anymore," said Peter.

"Ah, she'll get the message soon enough. She had big, ugly, hairy feet. Caroline had terrible breath. Amanda had skin like a crocodile. I just can't find the perfect woman. Now Alex, she is perfect,"

"Yeah, until you find something wrong with her. You need to stop being so shallow. Wait a minute, what was wrong with my wife that she wasn't perfect?"
"Absolutely nothing. I just wasn't ready to settle down then. Now I am,"

"Yeah, right!"

"Can you show me the machine in action?" Peter pushed the radar a few yards and explained the images on the display screen. They were more than likely pipes and cables under the layer of cement and soil. Stephen folded the machine and put it in the trunk of his car. It was a perfect fit.

"Thanks again. I'll see you in the morning. Cheerio,"

"I mean it Stephen. Be careful with it. I'll lose my job if you break it or lose it,"

"It's in safe hands. Thanks, Peter. See ye."

Chapter 11

"This will all be over by the morning Dad, I hope. Yes, I have everything I need to do this. Tell Kevin to keep it together, it won't be long now. Maybe you can stay in the church for the night to watch him. Because I'm afraid of what he might do. Hold on a minute, he's just a teenager who has no idea of what's happening and why. Dad, I'm in another country planning to commit a crime that could cost me a considerable amount of time of my future and it's all on your words, your guidance. So you better be right about this. I've had people here thinking I'm crazy. I had to tell them the truth, it was the only way they would help me. I have to go now. I'm shopping for equipment to help with the night time grave robbing. I'll ring you in the morning. Bye."

Sean hung up the phone, he felt uneasy. Kevin's behaviour was becoming increasingly erratic.

"What's wrong?" asked Alex.

"I just keep thinking this is foolish, how could this all be real? If I hadn't seen my son in a catatonic state, with a 'dark mass' flying around his room and in the pub last night, I wouldn't have believed any of this. There is a curse allegedly affecting our bloodline for generations. I thought all the years of hearing the wailing during the night, haunting me, was just my imagination playing tricks on me. I trust my Dad and love my son, that's why I'm her,"

"I can see you're dealing with a lot. I'm sorry. But as you said, it's going to be all over soon,"
They continued shopping in the hardware store and collected all the tools needed, including a large spade and a powerful UV torch. Sean worried Stephen would not be so prepared.

"Can you drop me back at the hotel please Alex?"
"I know… I'll drop the car at home and we'll get a taxi. No parking, remember? We can have dinner in the hotel. I do need to go to bed at a reasonable time if I'm to get up before dawn. A girl needs her beauty sleep,"

The mini struggled with the excess weight and just about made it to Alex's house. Sean jumped out so she could reverse it into the drive with ease. He waited outside as Alex gathered some belongings and changed her clothes. Loud voices came from the narrow council townhouse, an apparent argument over who would be minding her sister's children tonight. Not wanting to listen, Sean took a little stroll to find a taxi. Soon enough, a black saloon pulled in and the driver jumped out to help with the large bags.

"Jaysus. What's in there then? Are you burying a body? Yer not going to the Dublin Mountains are ye?" laughed the driver.

"No, only to dig one up," Sean remarked and winked at the driver.

Sean ordered the driver to stop outside the house as Alex stomped her way out.

"Is everything all right?"

"Fine. Family life is bliss, ye know. My sister needs a minder again while she goes out gallivanting with her new man of the month. My Mom will have to do it, but she wasn't happy because it's bingo night. They think I don't have anything better to do."

Sean was delighted to see the city centre again; it was closer than he thought. They trod up to his room and Sean ran the taps until it reached the right temperature and put the shower on. He was worried about what he was going to do, and hoped a rinse would make him more focused. Alex was watching television. Warm, soft water trickled down his face and chest. It was soothing, and his tense shoulders relaxed. Sean moved his shoulders in a circular motion until he heard a click. He then heard another click. It was the bathroom door opening and there stood Alex, naked. She glided over to him keeping eye contact at all times. Sean instantly became aroused. She placed her hand on the nape of his neck and pulled him closer to her.

"Are you sure about this?" he asked.
Alex didn't answer. She kissed him passionately and ran her hands down through the hairs on his chest and gently touched his nipples. Sean exhaled heavily with excitement. He was out of practice and constrained himself from coming too soon. This was difficult as the blood rushed around his body. Alex moaned with delight when he fondled her breasts and gently flicked her nipples. They didn't notice the shower starting to go cold. His hand slipped down between her legs and he rubbed until she was panting heavily, ready for him. Sean lifted Alex and positioned her against the cold tiles and entered her. Her arms were wrapped tight around his neck and he gripped the rail.

Alex's shouts of pleasure became louder and their motions quickened. Sean could feel the rush coming and was ready to climax. One last strong thrust and it was gone, both breathless and satisfied. He eased out of Alex slowly and gently kissed her lips. Sean had forgotten what it was like being this close to someone. His rebound relationship, after the separation, was a temp working at the school to cover a colleague's maternity leave. Carol was a cute brunette with ashen skin and eyes like chocolate Maltesers. It never would have worked, he knew she was too good for him, but enjoyed it while it lasted. Alex lay on his chest, he smelled her hair and thought of coconuts.

"Let's have dinner and then we can go to sleep, that's if you don't mind me staying with you tonight," said Alex.

"Of course I don't mind."

Hunger and thirst overcame them so they quickly so they dressed to leave and have some much needed nourishment. Alex impatiently pressed the elevator button many times. Sean grabbed her hand and affectionately held it. A small vacant elevator gradually glided down between floor two and one. Sean moved his attention upwards as a loud clunk sound came from above the elevator, where the cables are. The elevator shook violently for a few moments. They stumbled and held the rail for support.

Lights flickered and then went out. Sean used his phone to guide him to the controls and continually pressed the alarm button. Alex screamed.

"Is that you? I felt someone touch me,"

"No, it's not me."

The emergency light came on and hummed. Visibility was still limited, nevertheless Sean could make out the reflection of the large grey cloak hovering behind Alex. He directed his mobile towards the rear of the elevator, yet no figure appeared to be behind her. He stood back and stared at the image again. The Banshee was only appearing within the mirror itself. A scrawny rotting hand emerged, like from a pool of water, with skin flaking and transparent, showing dark putrid flesh underneath. Alex trembled and was unable to move. The Banshee reached for Alex. Sean heaved her stiff body towards him and the doors. He instructed her to press the ground floor button as he physically forced the doors open with his hands.

Blood poured from his middle finger when the nail cracked halfway. Lights from the lobby radiated through the opening and lit up the elevator. The hotel manager ran from the desk to aid the weary couple. They were only a few inches from the ground and squeezed through with just a small step down.

"What happened? Are you both okay?" asked the manager.

"Yes, we're fine. You need to have the elevator checked. We pressed the alarm and nothing happened. It was just lucky we were close to the floor and the flimsy doors opened," Alex whimpered into Sean's jacket.

"We're so sorry, sir. I will have it investigated straightaway. Please let us tend to your injury and you can have dinner in our restaurant compliments of the hotel. Again, sorry sir and madam."

The manager held up his hand and clicked his fingers. All available staff came to his attention, one with a first aid kit to clean and tend to Sean's bloody finger. Another escorted Alex to the seating area and provided a cup of water.

"I'm fine now, thanks," Sean advised the desk clerk. He could barely return Alex's nervous stare. Guilt filled his soul for the danger he had put her in.

"I'm dreadfully sorry Alex, this is entirely my fault. It was that horrid Banshee in the lift. It could have hurt you and this is not even your problem. I understand if you want to go home," he said.

"I'm not giving up now. I said I'd see this through and I will. I'm with you till the end," Sean put his arms around her and squeezed tightly.

"Thanks Alex. C'mon, let's order the most expensive food on the menu. Even if we have lost our appetite."

The hotel porter entered the elevator and jammed the door open with his foot. He pressed the alarm button. The ringing sound could be heard inside and all through the lobby. Repeating the test over and over again, the bell would sound each time. The porter shrugged his shoulders and ineptly returned to his post at the door.

Chapter 12

Brendan dozed off, he wanted a nap before heading back to the church for the night. It was obvious he would not get much sleep there. It was chilly in the house and, even with a cardigan, he felt the cold go through to his ageing bones. The letter box vibrated in the wind, snapping closed each time.

Brendan awoke with a jerk, someone banged heavily using the brass knocker on the front door.

"Sean, open the door. I know you are in there. The lights are on and your car is outside. Where is my son? Where's Kevin? Kevin, can you come and open the door please?"

"Oh no," Brendan whispered 'Claire,'
He had been avoiding her calls all day and advised Kevin to do the same.

Claire peeked into the front window through the gap in the curtain and spotted Brendan trying to hide behind his old rocking chair.

"I can see you Brendan. Open the door or I'll call the police. How's that for an incentive?"

"I'm coming, I'm coming. Hold yer horses,"

Brendan struggled to the door, holding his lower back with his hands and pressing into the muscle he had just overstretched. He had not moved that swiftly in years. Claire pushed her way in when the door opened.

"I've been ringing the three of you all day and not one of you answered. Where is Kevin? I want to bring him home if he is not well, where I can take care of him,"

"There is going to be a bit of a problem with that. He's not here. Now before you lose your temper. He's safely tucked away with Father David around the corner,"

"What? He's in bed with a priest?"

"No, no. That's not what I meant. Will you let me finish? He is staying in the church to keep safe. He is in serious danger,"

"From what? What are you going on about? Where's Sean? I want to talk to him now,'

'He's in Dublin. Just sit down and let me explain," he pleaded.

Starting with the dreams Kevin recently experienced, Brendan reminded Claire of his family curse. She refused to believe and called it nonsense. He then explained how the Banshee was haunting Kevin in his room and who knows how far it would have gone if he and Sean had not reacted so quickly.

"He's been in Dublin since yesterday, researching the Banshee and talking with the gypsies to find out about curses. Sean has located the whereabouts of the remains and will be digging for them in a few hours. So don't worry, Kevin will be back with you tomorrow."

"This is preposterous. How can you, as a sensible person, believe in this supernatural tripe?'

"Seeing is believing, Claire. We saw it. You can't change our destiny. Sean is doing what he has to do to save Kevin."

"You're right. Seeing is believing. So let me see my son. Take me to him right now. I want to make sure he is doing ok," Claire demanded.

"I was on my way there anyway to stay with Kevin. He's getting cabin fever, so I thought I would be a good Grandfather and keep him company."

Brendan flustered about the kitchen, bedroom and bathroom gathering his belongings and put them into a bag. He also sneaked in a small bottle of whiskey, hiding it under everything else. It would be the only help to get through the night. While Brendan was upstairs, Claire called Sean's mobile again.

"It's Claire again. Now I know why you haven't answered my calls all day. That's it Sean, the final straw. Kevin will not be staying with you and your Dad again. While you're off gallivanting in Dublin, your father is putting wacky ideas into our son's head about curses and the Banshee. I'm taking him home right now, away from this nonsense. I expect a sincere apology from you when you get back tomorrow, so see you then."

They left without saying a word to each other. Brendan was acting sheepishly, he had heard some of the message she left on Sean's phone and felt responsible for her reaction. He did not expect Claire to put a stop to Kevin from staying over again. Sean would be furious with him.
The tension was obvious as they made their way into the church. Brendan passed the altar and he knelt to bless himself, muttering words in honour of his God.

An embellished tut and sigh escaped Claire's mouth and she turned her back on him, folding her arms impatiently and tapping her foot on the thin red carpet, dirty and worn. People scarcely filled the varnished pews that clashed with the bright yellow walls and faded stained glass illustrative windows.

Large cobwebs attached to the high white ceiling swayed back and forth like the ebb and flow of a tide, ever reaching closer and closer to their destination. The last time Claire stepped inside a church, Kevin was being christened. Sean emotionally blackmailed her to do this, to follow his family's tradition. She classed herself as an atheist.

Claire didn't mind telling people she was adopted as a baby and raised by overly logical scientists. They believed, at five years old, she had a right to know where she came from and who she was as an individual. It was evident, with her dark hair and eyes, she was not the biological child of a fair-haired blue-eyed couple. Her biological mother was a young Irish girl who fell pregnant out of wedlock and sent to Britain to give her away as soon as she came into this world. Society shunned upon a girl with child and not be married in Seventies Ireland. In her twenties, Claire traced her mother, Theresa, to a small area named Celbridge in County Kildare.

It was a quaint little village south of Dublin with a large Palladian house full of history, scenic grounds and an unrealistic story of a visit from Satan during a game of cards. And following the stereotypical Irish surroundings, there were five public houses on the main street and three more in the surrounding areas. Nervous about meeting Theresa for the first time, Claire wore her navy pin-striped suit and high-heeled shoes, only to have to fool around in a large back garden with all of her seven nieces and nephews.

Theresa married a pleasant local man and had three more children, two boys and a girl named Siobhan. Claire did not envisage such an immense family affair but she thoroughly enjoyed the week she had with her new 'other' family. Siobhan was planning a trip to London excited about meeting her nephew and brother-in-law. Claire and Siobhan became best friends and talked on Skype every week.

"It's this way," said Brendan.

Entering the basic living quarters, Claire studied the kitchen and dining area with disgust. It was not up to her standards of cleanliness. The scum around the kitchen sink made her feel a little nauseous.

"Kevin. It's your Mammy. Where are you dear?"

"Father David," Brendan called out.

Both emerged from their rooms. Father David prepared for the next service in the evening and wore his green vestment. Kevin appeared dazed and frail with just a vest and shorts on, his being entirely detached from reality.

"Oh, my dear boy. What have they done to you?"

"Nothin', we've done nothin' to him. This is not our doing. It is something more sinister. I keep telling you this. He needs to stay here with Father David. He is safe here,"

"He's not safe here. The bloody state of him, he like death warmed up. He is coming home with me. Grab your bag, Kevin. We're leaving right now."

Kevin returned to the room to gather his belongings as Claire and the others sat down at the flimsy pine table. The chairs were not much better, the entwined seat and back squeaked with the weight of each person. Brendan wobbled a little and held the table until he felt steady.

"Before anything else is said, I just want to inform you, I am unaware of what is going on. I'm serving a parishioner in need. Brendan came to me and asked for help. To take his grandson in for a few days. He seems a little lost in the world and not sleeping well. That is all I know. I have a service to give to my other parishioners in a few minutes, so this needs to be sorted quickly."

Brendan clutched Father David's arm and urged him with his eyes, "Please, Father, Kevin cannot leave here yet. You don't understand,"

"Oh, not this stupid curse again," Claire blurted.

"What curse? Kevin didn't tell me about a curse," said Father David.

"The Banshee. She cursed our bloodline and murdered many of the men in our past generations. I believe Kevin is her next victim. Sean and I have had our fair share of haunting from her. Kevin started with the dreams and then she actually materialised in his room. We all saw her. I suppose she has become stronger because of Claire's bloodline. She is Irish too, ye know. That's why my son Sean is in Dublin, he is trying to save Kevin's life,"

"It's a hard story to take in, Brendan. As a man of the cloth and a believer of good, I also have to accept evil exists, no matter in what form. Claire, are you sure Kevin cannot stay here another night? What harm could it do?"

"This is ridiculous. I can't allow myself to believe this shit. I'm taking him home now. Kevin, are you ready?"

Kevin came out of the room with his bag draped over his shoulder. He was fully clothed now and felt a little better. Everyone stood up and made their way through the church. Brendan shook his head in disbelief. He braced himself for the worst. Father David waved at the congregation, advising he would be back in a few minutes to start the Mass. Kevin was first to reach the doors except he hesitated to open them and stepped back. Claire pushed past him and opened the heavy doors. Pulling him by the hand, down the four steps, they felt the cold breeze from the night sky envelop around them like a blanket of ice.

Brendan begged Claire not to take him yet. They were face to face, arguing with each other and Kevin kicked whatever pebbles he could find onto the road. Father David grew impatient and glanced at his watch. He then gazed at the sky to see the stars twinkling, some brighter than others. He followed the path of the Big Dipper to the houses across the street. Something moved on one the rooftops and caught his eye, but he couldn't make it out. It was much too big to be a cat. It glided so eloquently across the slates like a dark shadow running from the hot sun. Father David squinted hoping to see more clearly. It did not help with focusing on the dark mass getting closer.

Moving swiftly down the front of the house like liquid it quickly stood to attention in the direction of the conflicting group, with only Father David in awe of this apparition. Instinct warned him of oncoming danger.

He attempted to interrupt Brendan and Claire with a simple 'excuse me', still cautiously maintaining a watchful eye on the figure closing in.

It was now opposite them and slithered closer with each moment. Unnoticed by Brendan and Claire, Father David grabbed Kevin by the arm and pulled him back towards the church steps. He stood guarding him. Kevin quaked when he saw what was crossing the street. He knew it was her.

"Stop, stop, quit it. Hey! You really need to get inside now," Father David shouted. "It's not safe out here."

"What?" Claire asked.

She followed the horrified glare of her son and fixed her eyes on the approaching ghostly figure. She was unable to see under the hood of the cloak yet the hairs on the back of her neck tingled as this figure, she could tell, was not normal. Brendan tugged her jacket and hauled her towards the gates and the entrance of the church.

Father David stood in front of all three quoting from the Bible, hoping to shield them from harm. He rummaged through his pockets until he found the green marbled rosary beads given to him by his mother on her death bed. Holding out the small crucifixion, a loud patronizing cackle came from the Banshee. Some of the congregation had heard the commotion and peeked out the open church door astonished by the events unfolding before them.

"Brendan, get him inside quick," ordered Father David.

"I'm trying, Claire help me."

The Banshee rose high into the air to target Kevin from above and plummeted towards him, shrieking as she did. Kevin hollered and crouched down wrapping his arms around his head. Brendan tried desperately to move him through the gates whilst Claire watched Father David move to cover Kevin. He could see the horrific face of the Banshee. Her skin was grey with dark sockets to surround black soulless eyes. Blue cracked lips encircled the brown and yellow protruding pointy teeth. When she opened her mouth to squeal again, her cheeks showed gaping holes with little white maggots gnawing at the remaining flesh that resembled gums. The reek of her being burned his nose and throat like inhaling fumes from a burning fire.

Father David screamed as she tugged his clothes and picked him up.

Brendan, with Claire now helping, frantically towed the rigid Kevin through the gates and onto hallowed ground. Removing his enfolded arms, Brendan slapped him hard across the face to awaken him from his trance.

"Kevin, you're okay now. Stand up boy, you're safe."

They now followed the actions of the Banshee with the priest as an angry growl emerged when she realised Kevin was no longer within reach. With the priest still in the grip of her bony hands, struggling to release himself, she moved towards the street between the parked cars. Father David's legs dangled and kicked the bumper of a parked car, smashing the light and denting the bodywork. A siren could be heard, just around the corner, and was coming fast. The large vehicle, manned with heroic firefighters, came hurtling down the street on their way to an emergency.

The Banshee immobilised the priest by clutching his throat and squeezing the windpipe until he turned purple, struggling for breath. She saw the kindness in his heart and despised it. To her, he glowed like a beacon of righteousness. His death must be swift as goodness can spread quickly.

The fire engine was closing in, pressing the horn sporadically to warn the public of the potential danger. Propelled in front of this moving beast, Father David was struck down and ruptured like bubble wrap under the hefty tyres. His entrails sprawled down the road. The cars were splattered with a deep red liquid.

Crowds gasped, holding hands over their gaping mouths, and fleeing the scene. Deafening screeches cloaked the once quiet street. Curtains twitched continually from the surrounding houses and the Banshee vanished into the shadows.

Four burly men stepped down from the carriage to see the devastation. One stayed to radio the station requesting an ambulance and informed the chief of their failure to reach the emergency and to send another team. Distraught and confused, the firemen covered the bulk of the remains from view of the unfortunate bystanders and dared not approach them to inquire about how the religious man came to his untimely demise. An ambulance arrived soon after with two police cars following. A crowd had gathered which gave Brendan, Claire and Kevin an opportunity to disappear.

They pushed their way through to the church doors. Those at the back, who had not seen the atrocity, asked questions 'What happened? What did you see?' which were ignored.

"Quickly, we must get out of sight before this escalates and we are dragged to the local police station for questioning. Nobody knows who we are so they may start searching elsewhere. Hopefully they won't find us until morning, at least. That's all the time we need," said Brendan.

"What if they do look for us here? Kevin is not safe outside of these grounds. I can't let him leave,"

"We wouldn't be in this mess if you had listened to me in the first place. That good man out there would not have lost his life protecting the boy who you, only now, say cannot leave,"

Claire stood silent, overwhelmed by the blood on her hands of a noble man of God.

"I know and I'll have to live with it for the rest of my life. But my son is alive and if it came to a choice, I would still choose him,"

Tears trickled down her cheek. It was a harsh to say yet Claire meant every word. She turned her head to hide the shame. Kevin sobbed in the corner of the kitchen.

"Well, we can't undo what's been done. Only Sean can change the future. I'm going to ring him now. He needs to know what happened."

Brendan left the room to make the call. He didn't want to have this conversation in front of his grandson. Kevin was upset enough and he did not want to rub salt into his wounds.

"Hello Sean. It's me. I have some bad news. She murdered the priest. Yes, he's dead. Kevin is fine, physically. Mentally? He's on his last legs. She threw him under a truck. Well, at the moment it comes across as a terrible accident, but if they talk to anyone, it won't be good for us. We're going to stay here. Where the fuck else can we go? Exactly, if we leave now Kevin is at risk and we can't take that chance. So, I expect you to work fast. Right, ring me as soon as you can. I don't think I'll be getting any sleep tonight. Be careful, her wrath is also for anyone who gets in her way. Please, take care son."

When Brendan returned, Claire was comforting Kevin, telling him everything was going to be fine. Brendan wondered if she believed her own words.

"Well? Explain to me, what is Sean doing to stop this?"

"Don't start again Claire, he's doing everything he can for Kevin. Just because you can't see or understand what he is doing, doesn't mean he is not doing anything,"

Claire opened her mouth to respond but Kevin interrupted.

"Mum, please. Stop!"

Kevin had not said a word for many hours, so when he spoke Claire listened and stayed quiet. They sat in silence for quite a long time. The breeze could be heard seeping through the window frames and there came a heavy knock on the door.

Chapter 13

Sean held Alex, her arm draped across his chest and she slept peacefully. Even without make-up, she was pretty. Sean, unable to sleep for more than ten minutes at a time, heard a vibration come from his pocket, his Dad was ringing his phone. It must be important to call at this time. Slipping from Alex's embrace, Sean raced to answer before voicemail clicked in.

Bad news, Father David was dead. Asking what would happen now, Sean panicked to hear they had nowhere else they could go. If Kevin left the church grounds he would be killed.

"Okay. I'll ring as soon as possible. I can't risk going until it is nearer daybreak. I will Dad, I promise. Bye."

Sean returned to bed, not knowing if he would sleep yet knew he had to. A lot of energy was needed for digging. It was now eleven o'clock and they were due to rise, in just over three hours to meet Stephen.

The alarm buzzed loudly on the bedside table. Sean pressed the snooze button. He sat up not realizing where he was. He rubbed his eyes, focused on his surroundings, and finally came around to notice Alex still beside him.

"Alex, wake up. We have to get ready to go,"

"Five more minutes," she mumbled.

In the bathroom, Sean splashed ice cold water on his face. He shuddered. It the either the cold or what they had to do next. He didn't know.

"Alex, c'mon wake up. We need to get organised.

We've to meet Stephen in twenty minutes,"

"Yep, sorry, getting up now,"

Sean searched through his bag for clothes. He never thought he would be grave digging while here so opted for his trainers, sweat pants and a plain jumper.

Alex was out of bed and ready within minutes. She packed all their equipment into the large black bag. Sean thought it best to check out now and gathered all his belongings into his travel bag.

"Will you be leaving today? Back to London I mean,"

"I have to, my father and Kevin will need me. It's his birthday remember. I promised I'd bring him for his first legal pint," Sean said with tears welling up in his eyes.

"And you will. How about I come over in a few weeks? And you can take both of us out for a drink,"

"Really? What a great idea. Thanks Alex,"

Sean assumed he was just a little fling for Alex. He thought he would never see or hear from her again. At home in London, he felt lonely but here he felt part of something with Alex, a feeling he had not experienced for many years now.

"Let's go. Can you text Stephen please while I check out? We need to make sure he's on the way,"
"I will," she replied, taking out her phone.

It was chilly outside and being early on a Wednesday morning, not many people or cars were about. They waited at the side of the road for Stephen to arrive.

Two patrolling police officers passed by and studied the pair holding a large bag with spade handles protruding out. Although Sean saw them take notice, he remained aloof and carried on as normal. He did not want to attract their attention.

"Where is he? He's late,"

"He was on his way a few minutes ago. Harold's Cross is not too far away, we won't be waiting much longer," replied Alex.

Just as Alex finished her sentence, a white Audi pulled up in front on them. Sean courteously opened the front passenger door for Alex, suggesting she sit there to help with directions. The equipment bag was thrown into the back with Sean.

"Good 'early' morning, are we all ready for this?" asked Stephen.

"Not really," replied Sean.

"Well, you better get ready. Here's a copy of an old map of the area and its hand drawn so I don't know how accurate it is but at short notice, with little time to research, it's the best I could do. But at least it won't be a stab in the dark, right? Not with the radar machine. I've put a red ring around the original location. Alex, we are even now, right?"

"Yes, Stephen, we're even,"

Sean curiously asked what the last comment meant,

"Oh, nothing. Stephen just owed me a favour and that's why he's helping. Let's just leave it there, shall we?,"

Sean examined the map. He closed his eyes to try and visualise the hills and place the Stone of Destiny where it used to be.

"Are you tired, Sean?" Stephen spotted Sean in his rear-view mirror.

"Yes, but that's not why my eyes are closed. I'm picturing the Hill of Tara in my head, trying to place the Stone,"

"Maybe food and drink will help. I can't think straight on an empty stomach. I brought sandwiches and a flask of coffee. They are in the picnic bag on the floor behind my seat. Help yourself,"

Stephen came prepared much to the gratitude of Sean and Alex. Pouring coffee into small plastic camper cups was a difficult task in a moving vehicle but Sean managed quite well. With the caffeine in his body, he felt able to concentrate.

He studied the map again and realised where the Stone had been before being moved.

"Damn. I believe we have a problem," Sean shared the map with Alex. "Look! I think she is buried here. This is where the excavation is, exactly where all the fencing has been set up,"

"So, we move a few fences, no big deal. We're illegally grave-digging on a heritage site, I don't think adding the moving of construction material really measures up. Don't you think?" said Alex.

"I suppose."

Stephen saw flashing lights in his rear-view mirror and then came the short burst of the siren.

"Oh shit, the Gardai. Don't panic. They are probably checking for drunks on the road at this time of the morning. Everybody stay calm and follow my lead," The officer strolled up to the window and pointed a flashlight in Stephens's face, which impaired his vision.

"Hello Officer, is there a problem?" he asked with a cheeky grin.
"Yes, Stephen, there is,"

"Oh! Hi, Isabelle. What a coincidence meeting you here or is it?"

"You never returned any of my calls or messages,"

"Sorry, I've been really busy with work and I was going to give you a call this weekend,"

"Hmm, for some reason I don't believe you. So where are you off to at this time?" Isabelle shone the torch at the other occupants in the car and the equipment bag. The light stayed on the bag longer than Sean wanted, "What's all that for then?"

"We're going grave-digging," Stephen said, followed by a smile.

Sean gripped his knees and gritted his teeth, he wondered what the hell Stephen was up to.

"Now you're pulling my leg. I'll have to breath test you. My partner, in the car, is expecting me to do so. Can you blow in here, please? Don't stop until I say so,"

Stephen blew as hard as he could until he heard the beep when instructed to stop. The reading was clear.

"See, I am a good boy,"

"Some of the time. Now are you going to explain where you are going at this time of the morning with all that equipment or do we have to do this down at the station?"

Wiping the sweat of his brow, Sean tried to see how serious Isabelle acted. From what he could make out she had fair hair tied back into a bun with large blue eyes. She was tall with a slight build and an obvious needy persona.

"Well, Sean behind me here is a friend of Alex, over from the UK with the ashes of his Irish grandfather who recently passed away. On his death bed, he had one final request... to be brought home and buried under the same tree that he planted when he was just a wee boy at his family home in Meath. That's what the shovels are for. The reason we're doing it so early is because Sean has a flight to catch this afternoon back home so has limited time. I was kind enough to offer a lift because I'm just that kinda guy. You know, sweet, always willing to help,"

Stephen gave Isabelle another cheeky grin. Her partner called out for her return, it seemed they had a more urgent call to respond to.

"Well, I suppose it sounds like a plausible reason. On your way and unless I get a call from you soon, we may meet like this again and you might not be so fortunate,"

"Yes, officer. As long as you can wear your uniform outside working hours," Stephen said with a wink.

Isabelle paced back and they sped off with the siren continuously ringing.

"Are you fucking crazy? What were you thinking of telling her all that?" asked Sean.

"Hold on a second, what are you worrying about? The fact I told the truth with a smile, I knew it wouldn't raise suspicion. So I think you should be thankful, mate. Unless you wanted to be taken to the local station for meaningless questions and waste your time,"

"Okay, sorry, I'm just nervous,"

Not much was said in the car from then on, except Alex telling Stephen which way to go. They were now at their destination with not a sinner in sight. Silence filled the air like the brief space of time between the flash of lightning and the grumble of thunder, a build-up of static energy waiting to be released. Moonshine gave a bright glow to their surroundings which made it easier to see. Stephen carried the radar machine and Sean swung the bag over his shoulder. Alex tightly wrapped her hands around her arms and moved them up and down hoping to warm up. Offered an old red and black tartan picnic blanket from the car, Alex accepted gratefully and wrapped it around her head and shoulders with only her eyes and nose protruding. Out came the fluorescent torches from the bag to guide their way through the thick, overgrowing grass.

"What is that smell?" asked Stephen, holding his sleeve up to his nose to block the stench.

"Sheep shit. It's everywhere, so you might want to watch your step," said Alex.

"Thanks for the advice. I'll take note when I put my hundred quid shoes into shit. I see you are both well prepared," he said, scrutinising their feet and noticing the old attire they had on.

Sean ignored him not wanting to have a petty argument about shit just as he was about to dig up the remains of a person that had cursed his family for generations.

They followed the narrow path around the church grounds. Every step weighed heavily on Sean's shoulders. He imagined her remains, encased in some laboratory, enduring carbon testing or even an autopsy, depending on the condition. Even with the frosty air, sweat poured from his forehead. Alex sensed his uneasiness.

"Are you okay?" she asked.

"I'm as good as can be expected. I just don't know what I'll do if the remains are not there,"
"Let's cross that bridge if we come to it."

Sean was correct, fencing surrounded the mound they needed to dig near, however it was not difficult to move. One heave and the two men had the mound exposed. Sean held the map under the light of the torch and turned it around until he felt comfortable it faced the right direction. Sauntering around, Sean finally stopped at the base of the mound and knelt down to touch the ground and check the density. He was relieved it had softened from the rain all afternoon.

"Stephen, can you please check the ground here first? This is where she should be but considering the earth can slide over time, I recommend checking three or four feet in each direction,"
Stephen unfolded and switched on the radar. Loud beeps rang out when the screen came to life. They paused for a minute to scope the area to ensure they did not disturb anyone with the noise, but no lights came on, everything stayed dark and quiet.

"I wasn't expecting that," said Stephen.

"Clearly not," responded Alex. "It's lucky there is no one around here, you would wake a whole neighbourhood,"

Although new to the machine, Stephen confidently pushed the radar slowly over the ground, reading each and every symbol on the screen. It took several minutes in each direction to make his way four feet out from the starting point at the foot of the mound. When he was in the southeast direction he brought the radar to a halt and viewed the images. Stephen started again and followed the same direction for another five feet.

"I think I have something here. The digital signal processing system has detected a difference in the subsurface. It's about four feet down and in this direction. As it's about five feet long, this gives an indication as to what it might be. It has to be the place,"

He made marks on the ground to show the start and end points.

"Right, thanks Stephen. I'll start digging here."
Sean rolled up his sleeves and pushed the spade down with his foot to get as deep as possible and threw the first pile of soil over his shoulder. After about thirty minutes, Stephen observed Sean getting tired as he moved much slower now, taking a breather every couple of minutes to have some water. He stood out of the hole, wiped his face in his sleeve and stretched his sore back. Sean felt middle-aged for the first time in his life.

Alex kept watch by walking around the area and shining the torch on anything that moved, including the sheep who scarpered when the light came their way. Sean worried for her safety and checked her presence often. His fear for her started when she was under threat in the elevator, and then he heard about the priest. Brendan always assumed it was just their family at risk, but they both understood now they were wrong. The Banshee would hurt anyone in her way. Stephen interrupted Sean's thoughts.

"Let me give you a hand and take over. I'm freezing and feel guilty here watching you do all the hard work, plus I'm a little younger. I should be able to quicken up the pace."

Sean grunted yet gladly handed the spade over, he felt exhausted. The hole was now about three feet long and two feet deep. Stephen started off strongly made good progress with the hole, another two feet deeper and longer within fifteen minutes.

"I've hit something."

Sean signalled with his torch, turning it on and off whilst pointing it in Alex's direction. Not noticing the light, Alex closely followed what she saw moving in the woods.

What appeared to be a large piece of cloth, shimmered in the moonlight, and moved from tree to tree. She only ever caught sight of the corner of the figure before it disappeared into an abyss of blackness between the thick trees. Each time it came into view, the torchlight was not fast enough to catch a glimpse. Alex shuddered and felt the hairs on the back of her neck tingle. Instinct told Alex there was something wrong. Both men were now in the pit using their hands to dig out what Stephen had hit with the spade. They clawed at the dirt with haste like dogs burrowing for a meaty bone. Their nails turned black as they threw masses of dirt and stones over their shoulders. Sean felt thick material and used a small pocketknife to rip through what seemed to be a rug. Remnants of a skeleton lay before them. Alex stumbled over and gasped when she saw the remains Sean gathered in his arms.

"There's something in the woods. I don't know what it is but I have a bad feeling," said Alex.

"Quickly, get the large UV light from the bag," Sean said.
He stepped out of the hole with his arms full of bones.

"I'm sure it's just an owl or squirrel you saw," said Stephen.
Sean recognised a muffled howl came from the trees and it frightened him. "It's her."

Chapter 14

Brendan's hand trembled when he clasped the handle to open the door. "Hello officer. How can I help you?"

"I'm Detective Constable Brady from CID. We'd like you to help us with our inquiries. I know it's the early hours of the morning, but I saw the lights on and we need you to come down to the station to answer some questions. We have witness statements that don't make sense, yet they all conclude the unfortunate incident that occurred outside the church earlier was not entirely accidental nor self-inflicted,"

"Oh really! Well, I didn't actually see much and what we saw has distressed my daughter-in-law. She's inconsolable, so I don't think a trip to the station will do her any good,"

"And the young man, what did he see?" asked the police officer.

"What young man? There's no young man here, I think you must be mistaken,"

"The witnesses tell me a completely different story. So what are you doing here? Visiting Father David, were you, so do you mind telling me what is keeping you here now?"

DC Brady played with his notepad as he awaited their response, he expected to hear lies, and lies is what he did.

"As I said, my daughter-in-law is upset, so I didn't want to take her through the spectacle outside with all those people out there and the mess on the road. You know what I mean,"

"Can I come in and take a little look around? I need some personal details about the Father. Like his next of kin and his superior. I'm sure they'd like to know what has happened and to send someone over to maintain the place,"

Brendan wiped the sweat from his brow caused by the adrenalin now teeming from skin pores all over his body.
"Sure. Come in,"

Brady entered the kitchen to meet a woman chewing her nails to the stub. Her behaviour seemed odd. Claire did not make eye contact which Brendan knew would only make matters worse.

"This is my daughter-in-law, Claire McNeal," Brendan introduced her to DC Brady.

"Hello there. How are you feeling?" he asked.

"I'm okay. A little traumatised by the whole situation," she slurred, not willing to talk much more.

"So, can you tell me what happened?"

"Eh, not really. It all happened so fast. One minute he was standing there and the next he was under the fire engine. I can't really tell you much more than that," she said.

"And when you say 'us', who else was there with you?"
"My ex-father-in-law and..." Claire emphasised the 'ex'.
Brendan cringed as he thought she might fault under the pressure of police questions. For one second he begged the passing soul of Father David to aid in this deception for the sake of another life.

"... the churchgoers who stood watching," she said. Brendan quietly sighed with relief and thanked the heavens above.

"Watching what exactly? This is the missing piece of the puzzle I still need to be made aware of."
Brendan interrupted. "It's my fault, all of this is my fault. It's my drinking you see. My son and his wife. Ex-wife. They are worried about me and suggested I get the help of God and the Church. I was doing well for a while until I recently gave into temptation, God bless my soul, and relapsed. Claire insisted Father David be told, even though I begged her not to, and that is what the crowd saw."

"And the young man, who is he?" asked DC Brady.

"I told you already, there is no young man with us. They are mistaken," Brenden was stating to lose his patience now.

"Where is your son? Is he also a witness?"

"No, no, he's in Dublin on business,"

A noise came from beyond the kitchen, the clicking of a door being gently closed, "Who is that then?"

"Ah, must've been the breeze," answered Brendan, "It's an old building."

"Right, I need to find Father David's personal belongings. Can you direct me to an office?" DC Brady pointed to the back rooms.

"There's no office here. It's a desk in his bedroom. Follow me,"

They left the kitchen with Brendan humming a sorrowful song to hide other sounds possibly coming out of the other room. Brendan left the officer to do his job and returned to the kitchen.

"Brendan, I feel terrible lying to an officer of the law," Claire whispered.

"If you don't want Kevin to be her next victim, or us, you need to keep your mouth shut. Our story is working, for now. Once he continues to believe it, we're in the clear and won't have to leave, well, hopefully not in the next few hours."

Hearing Brady's muffled voice, and assumed he was notifying people of the terrible news on the phone, Brendan slipped into Kevin's room. Kevin was not to be found.

"Kevin. It's your Granddad. Where are you?" he whispered.

A slight tapping noise came from the closet as Kevin unlocked the door from the inside, "Good boy, Kevin. It all seems to be going well. He is asking us to go to the station, but I think we should be able to stay. If we do have to go do not make any noise. Wait here until we can come back."

"I don't want to be left here alone. Please, don't go, don't leave me," he cried.

"You'll be fine, just stay put. Trust me."
"Okay, Granddad."

Brendan closed the closet and Kevin locked the door again. As he left the room, Brady left Father David's room.

"I found an open window causing this door to rattle. I thought it best to close it. Did you find the details you needed?"

"Yes, thanks."

Brendan expected Brady to follow him back to the kitchen. Instead, he entered the other room.

"This is just the spare room, officer. There's no one in here," he said loudly.

"Just call me Brady. I can check it for myself," Brady circled the room and tested the only window, "This window doesn't open," he said.

"What? Eh, well, I just made sure it wasn't open. But the frame is so old, it still lets a breeze in. Do you want a cup of tea?"

"No, thank you,"

He continued to examine the room by feeling the temperature of the bed, checking the drawers of the bedside table and attempting to open the closet. Twisting and turning the handle Brady forcefully pulled and pushed the door but it would not open.

"Father David must have it locked for a reason. Maybe for the church bits and pieces,"

"In the spare room, I don't think so,"
Brady pressed his ear against the door. Kevin had heard what they said so far and dared not move, not even to breathe, knowing the officer suspected something.

"So, can you both come to the station later today and give a statement of the events?"

"Of course Officer Brady. We'll go to my house and get some sleep, I'm exhausted, and then we'll go to the station to make a statement in the morning. I'll say it again I didn't see much. I was too busy minding Kev... Claire,"

"Why would Claire need minding? You said 'you' had the problem,"
"Well, she was upset I was drinking again so I tried to reassure her I wouldn't fall off the wagon for a second time,"

"Right, I think I've heard enough. I'll just take all your details then I'll go,"
Sitting at the table, Claire observed Brady incessantly play with his pen by holding it between his two fingers and in his mouth.

"Do you smoke?" she asked DC Brady.
"Unfortunately, I do."
"Can I have one please? I don't think I ever needed a cigarette as much as I do now,"
"Claire, you quit a long time ago, please don't," Brendan begged.
"Mind your own business Brendan, I'll have one if I want,"

Brady reluctantly handed Claire two cigarettes. He could hardly refuse a simple request only just to add, "I hope you won't smoke them in here,"

Brady finished taking all their details and stood up to leave. Another noise came from the back again. Dashing to the spare room with Brendan hot on his heels, he pushed the door open. The closet was slightly ajar now, and Brady glanced at Brendan with disapproving eyes. He pulled the closet door open. Kevin rested on the floor with his knees pressed into his chest. Guilt was written all over his face, his puppy dog eyes glared up. Brady noticed his eyes were sore and red from crying.

"It's my fault Father David is dead,"
Brady stood back and directed Kevin to the kitchen with one stern finger signal.

"You all have some explaining to do, especially the reason for lying to a police officer,"
Claire dashed to her son's side as DC Brady escorted him to a chair.

"Oh, Kevin, are you all right? Leave him out of this, he's innocent," Claire shielded him from accusations.

"You involved him by lying to me. So what I need to understand is why?" DC Brady eyes flickered on all three.

"You wouldn't believe me if I told you," said Brendan.
"Try me."

Chapter 15

Alex frantically searched for the button to switch on the large UV light. "I'm telling you, it sounded like an owl to me, or maybe an owl catching an unfortunate animal and it shrieked with terror when caught," Stephen said holding back a tone of mockery.

Sean dropped all the bones into a small bag. Not wanting to miss any, he raked his fingers through one last time. Something metal caught on his index finger, he pulled it out easily and held it up in front of his face in the glow of the torch. What was shaped like a fish hook, until he cleared the debris from it, was an odd charm on the end of a necklace. Sean put it into his inside pocket.

"I have them all. Let's move quickly to the church grounds,"

Under direction from Sean, Alex now circled the group, shining the light in every direction. Amused by their actions Stephen casually watched the frenzied duo fuss over bones and torches.

"I'm putting the radar back into the car and will catch up with you in a few minutes. You're finished with it, right?"

"Stephen, please don't leave the group. The light is the only protection we have. Otherwise she would have attacked and killed us by now,"

"You know I'm here as a debt I owe to Alex, and I've pulled a rabbit out of a hat for you, but I'm not buying into all this shit. If you want to fool yourself and a trusting, lovely woman into believing in curses, retribution and ghosts, go ahead,"

Sean moved closer so not to be overheard.

"Please, I'm begging you. Alex doesn't know, but a priest died in London trying to protect my son. She kills anyone involved, anyone that gets in her way. Which could be you or Alex,"
"I'll take my chances."

He walked off laughing heartily and made his way out to the car park, awkwardly pulling the machine along the large tufts of grass.

Reaching his car, he stood facing the trunk and gazed at the reflection of the shimmering moon on the paintwork. This radiant image did not last as a dark shadow rippled across the natural light like a lunar eclipse darkening the sky. Stephen apprehensively observed a large bat-shaped obstacle soaring over the field then swooping down towards him. Quickly ducking, it narrowly missed his head. Stephen took to his heels and darted back to the ray of light he could see from over the wall. A loud cackle followed his every move. Each time it lunged to seize Stephen, he would plummet to the ground. Sean and Alex were cagily making their way to the church grounds with the bones and equipment after sloppily filling in the hole.

"Help!" yelped Stephen.

Alex shone the light around trying to find Stephen. He called for help again.
Blinded by the torch in his eyes, Stephen tripped and fell over. Behind him flew the Banshee. It screeched when hit by the UV rays and scarpered away.

"She's real. She tried to get me,"

"Quick, get over here," ordered Sean.

"What are we going to do?" Alex asked.

The Banshee saw her opportunity while Stephen stood unprotected. She grabbed his arms and hoisted him high into the air.

"Stephen, no!" howled Alex.

Stephen hollered as he saw the ground move further and further away from him. Sean and Alex watched helplessly as Stephen's squirming body hovered between the church's four steeples. Laughing as she let him drop, he believed he was being thrown to his death only to land on the rooftop. She enjoyed toying with him and floated beside him, her head down and hood covering her face. Stephen cowered on hands and knees into a shadowed corner.

The Banshee changed her appearance and became the endearing young woman. She beckoned him, singing her enticing lament. Like a moth to a flame, Stephen sauntered over, ogling the vision before him.

"No Stephen, don't. That's not the real her. Keep away," shouted Sean.

Sean said these words, yet knew it was hopeless to try and stop this man now. Stephen was in her clutches and they were helpless. Maybe if he was quick enough, he could stop her.
"Come on, we can only save him if we bury her bones on holy ground,"

Sean grasped Alex's hand and yanked her towards the entrance gates. She sobbed uncontrollably and felt responsible for including Stephen in what she thought was an adventure. She had cared for him deeply, they had become good friends and now sure to die. Sean dug into the ground with his bare hands, knowing he would only need to go a foot deep to fit all the bones. Alex was now helping.

Stephen caressed her hair and face; a vision of beauty and she wanted him, yearned for him. She sang to him. Brushing his fingertips on her lips, he wanted to taste them. He leaned in and tenderly kissed her, sucking her lips into his mouth and nibbling on them.

"Oh my God, he's kissing her now. Why would he do that?" asked Alex.

"He doesn't have a choice. She is singing to him and is now under her control. My son had similar dreams. She would sing and he would go to her, it's like being brainwashed,"

Sean continued to dig furiously to get deep enough. Just another minute, he thought. When he felt movement in his mouth and the echoing sound of laughter Stephen stopped kissing and spat into his hand.

Three maggots wriggled about on his palm and were soon covered in the vomit that pursued such a revolting sight. Stephen did not understand what had occurred and awoke from his coerced mind to see the horrific ghost pounce, to force him over the edge.

"He's stopped now and bent over. Oh shit, he's vomiting. Oh Stephen, stay away," said Alex.
Sean ceased digging. Alex handed him the bag and without even thinking Sean poured the bones into the hole.

"No... Stephen! She pushed him over!" roared Alex.

Sean's heart sank, he did not want to have another innocent person die. It was too late. Grappling at the wall on the way down, pain seared through Stephen's hands as the skin and nails caught on the walls and were torn asunder. For a brief moment, when he knew there was no way back, he pictured Alex in his mind. He did love her, but allowed his reputation to ruin his happiness. Now she would never know. Stephen hit the ground and death was instant with blood pouring profusely out of the back of his motionless head.

The Banshee relished in his death and swirled around squealing like a pig. She then turned to Sean and growled with hatred. She wanted him to be her next victim.

Sean kicked the little mound of earth over the obtruding bones and she cried out. Fading from view the Banshee knew she had missed the chance to seek revenge on those who impeded on her curse and wailed with disgust. Sun rays crept over the hilltop and the Banshee vanished, much to the relief of Sean. Alex ran to Stephen, to be with him, to hold him, to say 'I love you'. She checked his pulse with her fingers in the hope there might be a weak heartbeat. No pulse. Alex closed his eyelids, she could not bear to witness the lifelessness in his eyes. She held him in her arms and cried into his shoulder.

"Stephen, why didn't you stay with us? You tenacious fool."

"I'm so sorry Alex. I never expected anything like this to happen. We need to go."

"And just leave him here like this? We can't. I can't."

"Alex, if we stay and call the police they won't believe our story. What are we meant to say? A ghost killed him or it was an accident and he fell. They will doubt any story we have. But if it is believed he was on his own, they will think it's suicide. We can't change what has happened and I know you cared for him, but if we stay, we will be setting ourselves up for a fall, a hard one,"

"Okay, I know. But what about his car? If we drive it away, won't it seem odd?"

"We have to leave it here. It's daybreak now, we know which way we're going, so we'll have to flag a taxi or hitch a ride… once we get out of the area."

"Right then, it's a bit of a walk so we need to go now before we get any sign of humanity."

Alex kissed Stephen and said goodbye. They brought the equipment to dispose of on the way and Sean took his belongings from the car. They were weighed down, but not for long. There were plenty of bushes on the narrow, quiet country roads to hide the bag. Sean allowed Alex to walk ahead and phoned Brendan to inform him the ugly deed was done with one unfortunate casualty.

Although he was comforted to hear his grandson was now out of harm's way, he was troubled to know about another fatality. Brendan hoped Sean would not have to endure what they were going through now with the police. They were still being questioned after trying to conceal Kevin. DC Brady knew they were hiding something. Having made reasonable excuses as to what happened, the police officer remained unconvinced. He asked how Sean would deal with the event over there.

"I won't be. At the moment they'll think he jumped because she threw him off the top of a building. If they follow up on his movements from the early hours of the morning, and they will sooner or later, we'll be put in the picture. I'll be back home by then. I'm worried about Alex. Alex, I told you about her Dad, she has helped me through this whole situation. I am concerned. She will still be here and they will harass her. I'm going to book my flight in a little while. Yes, I'll be home as soon as possible. How is Claire holding up? She blames me for all this, doesn't she? I'll sit down with her when I get back and we'll talk through it. See you later. Thanks Dad, I owe you my son's life."

Sean jogged to catch up with Alex. He could tell she had been crying, "I hope one day you'll forgive me for what I have put you through."

She gave a little smile, "Stephen would be honoured to know he helped save a young boy even if it meant sacrificing himself. Although he let no one close enough to know, he had a big heart. I saw that side."

"I did too. I also see that side in you."

Sean wrapped his arm around her shoulders to comfort her. They were now near the main road and hailed a taxi to take them to Alex's house

Chapter 16

"Do you believe in the supernatural, the paranormal, DC Brady?" Brendan's question and glare made DC Brady uncomfortable.

"As a professional I am obliged to say no, but we all grew up with fears and stories we believed in. If you're gonna tell me what those witnesses said about a ghoul pushing Father David under the truck, is true, then you're wasting your breath,"

"That's what I was worried about. Unless you believe, our story means nothing to you. But you have no eye witness to say the three of us had any hand in what happened to the poor man. We were not near him at the time. Therefore, you have no evidence or witness account to charge us with a crime. It is your job to find this 'ghoul', not mine. Otherwise, you will probably have to record it as an unfortunate accident, with god-fearing overly sensitive witnesses seeing shadows and mistaking them for the work of the Devil."

"I don't like your tone Mr. McNeal. You're telling me a ghost did this, but because I can't charge any person, as no one was near him at the time, it'll have to be written up as an accident,"

"Yes, makes sense to me, to everyone. I'm not telling you how to do your job, but you can't report a bunch of bystanders said they saw a ghost push him, so you'll have to sugar-coat this regrettable incident,"

"Yes, I'm stuck between a rock and a hard place. Yet you can't stop me from hauling you all down the road for an interview,"

"And where would that get you? Our statements would be the exact same and you would be the laughing stock of the station. Think about it."

The guidance being forced upon him by a pensioner infuriated DC Brady. He thought carefully about what Brendan said. The old man was right, he could not force these people to tell a version of a story he wanted to hear. A story he did not agree with and he certainly could not report to his superiors what the witnesses believed killed the priest. He would probably be demoted and had worked so hard to get to his current rank.

It was not easy for him as he had not come from a law enforcement background. Most of his extended family, had, in fact, committed many crimes albeit misdemeanours, nothing too serious.

Alas, it had hindered his status in the workplace. A decision needed to be made on this perplexing scenario, he had two options. He could say it was an accident, and exclude the inaccurate paranoid religious followers' statements, and the investigation is over, or report a ghost did it. They had no evidence or video footage to say otherwise. To conclude a ghost murdered the priest would make him a laughing stock at the station. After gazing out the window for some time, with three apprehensive individuals, DC Brady had made a decision.

"Although I'd love to bring you all down to the station, and I hate to admit this, but you're right. I can't charge you with a crime and if I took an official statement on the story you are telling me I would probably be asked to hand over my badge. So, I am going with option one. The religious freaks saw shadows and invented an evil spirit they believed pushed the priest, but their imagination ran wild because he regrettably tripped and fell in front of the vehicle."

Claire was so glad to hear this, she squeezed Kevin tightly in her arms and he couldn't breathe.
"Mum, I still can't leave here,"
"Of course you can. I talked to your Dad in Dublin, he has done the deed. Her remains are now buried on holy ground and you're safe now. You can go home," added Brendan.

"I don't even want to know," and DC Brady left.

"Is Dad coming home?" yearning to see him.
"He should be home late afternoon, near evening time," Brendan ushered them to the door.

"Mum, you can let go now," Claire released the grasp on her only son, "I think you're forgetting something honey. Happy birthday!"
It just dawned on Kevin; he was now eighteen. He had been waiting for this day for weeks and when it arrived, the moment passed without noticing. Staying alive had overshadowed the important event, with good reason. Sean had promised to take him for his first legal pint in the local public house and he was excited about it now more than ever. Claire initially objected but she understood the bond they had and the need to release tension after such an ordeal.

"Sure, it's only a drink. The boy needs some normality after going through all of that!"
"Thanks, Granddad."

Chapter 17

Online at Alex's house, Sean booked his ticket home.
"Why do you have to go so soon?"
"It's my son's eighteenth birthday. What kind of father would I be if I stayed?"

"I know, I'm sorry. I just wish you could stay another day," Alex did not want to be left alone to deal with the aftermath; it would not be the end of this story.

When Stephen is found there would be questions and Alex knew they would knock on her door.
"I've booked my flight for four o'clock so I'll need to be there around three. We still have a good few hours together. Would you like go somewhere?"

"Like where?"

"I don't know, take me to your favourite place. Somewhere that means something to you."

"Okay. It's a place I used to go as a teenager hanging out with my mates."

Alex's family were rising from their slumbers and the bathroom was full of bustle with the shower and toilet being used, doors being slammed and alarm clocks thrown across rooms.

"It's best we go now then. I don't want my family seeing me in this state."
Quickly discarding her bloodstained clothes in the waste bin, Alex dressed in a half dry top and jeans from the clothes horse and another jacket from under the stairs. Slipping out the back door, they were able to leave before anyone in the house had the chance to come downstairs.

The Grand Canal started from the centre of Dublin and flowed all the way through Co. Kildare. Sean knew of this county as Claire's biological family originated from there and she had visited many times over the years. Suir Bridge wasn't much of a scenic area yet the canal greenery was quaint with black and white barges crossing over the 'old fashioned way' and a walkway to follow the water although the graffiti under the bridge did lessen the appeal. The ground cold and wet. They sat on the grass using some old newspaper from the car. Alex stared into the water in a daze and threw flower petals she had picked.

"It happened here, didn't it? Where your friend drowned,"

"How did you know?"

"Well, it's a nice place but hardly picturesque so it had to be somewhere that really meant something to you. I remember the story you told me in the pub,"

"This place was a turning point for me, in a fucked up kinda way. Had my friend not drowned here and brought me to my senses, I could be under the bridge shooting up or even dead from an overdose, who knows. The rocky path I was on crumbled, I feel lucky to escape, and I found a new path. I always come here when I am in conflict with my feelings or need direction,"

"So how do you feel now? You've been through a lot. Do you feel you've lost your way?"
"I don't even know if I have a way anymore. With Stephen dead, it made me realise how quickly we can go. Cliché, huh? I want to be at the end of my life and regret actions I've done instead of actions I haven't. Do you know what I mean?"

"Abso-fucking-lutely. That's why I want to travel to Asia. I want to do something worthwhile. My life started in school, then onto college, back to school, married, and then divorced. Being a father is an honour and raising Kevin was amazing, except I need something more,"

"I totally agree with you,"

"Well, if you really are, why don't you come with me? I mean it, come to Asia with me. We're compatible, we get on and I would love to get to know you more. So, will you?"
"Yes, I will."

They sat for a while talking about the future. Where Alex would like to go... Shanghai, Beijing, Tokyo. What Sean would like to experience... walking The Great Wall, riding in a rickshaw, climbing Mount Fuji. The list continued on and they giggled with excitement thinking of the possibilities.
"It's time. I have to go to the airport."

Time flew as they ate, drank and discussed arrangements in the airport bar. Sean would not need to work notice for his employers. He was suspended for two months and would not need to go back at all. Alex was to ask for her education venture to be put on hold and resume her course when she returned.

They turned to view the news being screened on the television behind them:

'The body of a thirty-six-year-old man was found today at the site of the Hill of Tara. An employee of the tourist office based in St. Patrick's Church, beside the famous heritage mounds, discovered the body early this morning when he arrived at work. The man is believed to be a member of the Trinity College Faculty. They are not seeking anyone in connection with the death, however, if you have any information that may help with the investigation you are urged to contact your local Garda station.'

"So they're not looking for anyone yet. How long will that last? No doubt the museum will be wanting the return of their radar machine and the question will arise 'what did he do with it and why?' Alex, it's best if we are over the other side of the world for this," Sean grew anxious. He didn't think it through. "Will the authorities not still want to talk with us?" Alex breathing quickened.

"Yes they will. Calm down. Breathe slowly. But what can we tell them, the truth?"

"I suppose. I don't like this part Sean, what will we say?" Her hand shook as she lifted a drink.

"We should stick to the near truth, it'll be easier. We were there for a comic 'ghost' hunt, you showing me a bit of Irish heritage. We left and pulled a taxi and he must have jumped. We don't know what he wanted

the radar machine for or why he committed suicide. Are you okay with that story?"
"I think so,"

Walking towards the departure gate, scores of businessmen and women hurried past to ensure they boarded first so their bags had a place in the overhead compartments. Families were crying goodbye to their educated young emigrating from a country now diseased by politicians and bankers' errors. Groups of football fans, drunk and causing a scene, swaggered along the crowd control barriers shouting and laughing.
"I hope they're not on my flight. I'm not in the right humour,"

"Just ignore them if they are. Will you call me later please? I need to know when to book my flights over,"
"Yes, I'll call you, but I need a few days to support Kevin and keep my head down with my ex, she'll be after my blood for a while. I also need to tell people our plans, which will not be greatly received either."
They kissed and said farewell, hoping the next few days would go quickly so they could be with each other again. He gave one last wave before going through the door.
Sean sent a text message to Brendan, while waiting to board, asking to be picked up from the airport. Brendan confirmed he would be there.

Chapter 18

Claire waited patiently in the car at Gatwick arrivals. Insisting she drove to collect Sean, Brendan eventually backed down. Claire was a stubborn woman not to be reckoned with. Checking her phone, she saw his flight had landed and stomped to the arrivals area. From a distance she spotted Sean having to push his way through the multitude of travellers.

"Sean, over here," she said, waving.
Seeing Claire disturbed Sean, he knew he was in trouble. Her arms folded as he approached and the tension was thick in the air.

"Hello, Claire,"
"Let's talk in the car, I don't want to make a scene in a public place,"
Sean carefully crafted his response and agreed on not having a debate there, it would be a debacle.

As they exited the arrivals area, Sean was blinded by the Sun which stretched over the buildings to reflect off the windows and glaze the footpaths. For Sean, it felt good to be home. Claire's car was not far away. She slammed her car door shut.

"How could you not tell me about this? He's my baby, Sean. Did you forget I've gone through thirty hours of labour to give birth to him? I raised him, nursed him, and nurtured him. If he was in danger I should have been the first to know. Instead, you shut me out and I inadvertently put Kevin in danger,"

"Will you let me speak before you continue? I'm sorry I didn't tell you. It all happened so fast and my Dad practically pushed me onto an airplane. I hoped it would only be for a day or two at the most except it ran into three. I didn't want to worry you unnecessarily. I found it difficult to believe myself so how would I convince you. Now, as his father, I have also raised him so don't forget it. It's a joint effort,"

It was tit-for-tat for the remainder of the journey. Who did what wrong, how the situation should have been dealt with and the terrible impact this would have on Kevin.

"Claire, we're wasting our energy arguing about this. Luckily, it's all over and Kevin is alive,"
"No thanks to you and your family,"

"Wait a minute. It's because of both our 'families' that we were in this mess. The curse has to be in your bloodline as well, you're of Irish descent too,"

"I know. I'm sorry. I wasn't thinking,"

"We're here now. Let's drop this and get along, for Kevin. It's his birthday for God's sake. All I want to do is see him,"

Brendan stood at the open door with Kevin directly behind him. They appeared to be so much happier since when he last saw them. The car had not even stopped when Sean jumped out and dashed up the garden path.
"I knew you could do it, son. Well done," said Brendan.

He patted Sean on the back as he came into the house.
"Thanks Dad, that means a lot,"

"Kevin," said Sean, holding out his arms, "thank God you're all right. Come here and give your old man a big hug," tears came to Sean's eyes, which he quickly wiped with his sleeve. "I am just so happy to see you. I was so worried."

"I'm okay, Dad, thanks to Granddad. Who knows what would have happened if he hadn't brought me to the church. And Father David," Kevin paused.

"Yes, I will thank him in a prayer tonight. He is with us in spirit and I'm sure he's proud he saved you. Religion is about the sacrifice you know," Brendan added.

"So Dad, tell me what you had to do in Dublin?" They all sat at the family table, with cups of tea and a whiskey for Brendan, while Sean told them of the account of his time in Dublin, from his research in Trinity to his experience with the Travellers. Kevin and Claire were shocked by the story of the bare-knuckle fighting, but Brendan said it happened all the time in Ireland. Sean decided not to inform Kevin and Claire of Stephen's death. Kevin felt guilty enough without letting him know someone else perished to save him. Telling the history of the Hill of Tara was greatly received by all, describing the mounds and the crowning of the High Kings of Ireland.

"I think you should go over to visit Dublin, Kevin. You'd really like it over there," said Sean.

"Will you take me there, please?"

"That's something else we need to talk about, but not today,"

"What's that then Sean? Are you moving over there now?" asked Claire.

"No, I am not. I didn't want to go into this today. I want to go travelling for a while. A few years maybe. Over to Asia to see the sights and find some work,"

"Oh really, are you going alone Sean?" asked Claire.

"That's not really any of your business Claire. We're divorced. Remember,"

"You may not be a husband anymore, but you're still a father. Re-mem-ber!" Claire took liberties when saying remember slowly.

Sean shuffled uncomfortably in his chair, this was the statement he had been waiting for. He knew his responsibilities as a father and abided by them for eighteen years.

"He's a young man now and doesn't need me around cramping his style,"

"I don't want you to go Dad, but you only get one life and you shouldn't waste it. Go do what you have to, sure I'll be here when you get back,"

"Thanks son, I appreciate 'your' support,"

"Ye fucker, what about me? I haven't that many years left you know. You'll be coming home to me funeral," said Brendan angrily.

"Aw, Dad, don't give me the guilt trip. You were complaining last week that I should hurry up and move out, that I was wrecking your head,"

"Yeah, I said move but not to the other side of the world. Ah, sure I wish you all the best, son. Are you going with that woman you met in Dublin?"

"Dad!" Sean cringed.

"Oh, right, I see now. You travelled over to Dublin to save our son's life, yet you found the time to meet someone over there and now you're going travelling with her. How conservative! Are you crazy Sean?" Claire asked.

"Not that I owe anyone an explanation. I didn't just meet her. She helped me figure all this out and we connected. She might change her mind and not go with me, I don't know. I have been planning this trip in my head for quite some time. I wanted to wait until Kevin reached a certain age. He's doing his A-levels and those bullying bastards have stopped. So I'm doing something for myself,"

Claire's sly comments eventually ceased as did the guilt trip from Brendan. It seemed they all accepted his pending departure. Sean did not back down and would not be told whether he could go or not.

Brendan sighed and offered to make dinner knowing they wouldn't be in the mood to eat the only dinner he makes, an English breakfast.

"No thanks, Brendan, we're off home," said Claire

"You are not. I promised to bring my son out for his first 'legal' pint in the local pub, and you're not changing my plan. So you can either stay here for a while or go home and I'll drop Kevin off at school in the morning,"

"I'm not going to school this week. I'm still upset by everything. I'll start back next week,"

Neither Claire nor Sean argued with him, he had been through a lot over the last few days and needed a rest. Claire decided to stick around and make dinner using the bits and bobs Brendan had in his pantry and fridge. Within minutes Claire called everyone to the table and served up delicious pasta and fried vegetables with a spicy tomato sauce. It always amazed Sean how she could cook up a mouth-watering feast using limited resources in a short space of time. He never questioned the magic and ate every last bit. Brendan patted his full stomach, he had not eaten healthily in a while.

"Fair play to ye Claire. That is the best meal I've had since my dearest wife passed away,"

"You're welcome, Brendan,"
Brendan leaned over and whispered into Kevin's ear.

"All women love to be complimented on their cooking," he said winking.

"Aww lovely, Mam, thank you." he shouted into the kitchen to earn brownie points.

The patter of rain echoed throughout the house as dusk settled in the night sky.
"Are we ready to go for a pint then?"

"Yes Dad, ready, willing and able! Do you need to have a shower?"

"Just a quick one. I'll be ready in five minutes,"
Standing under the water, Sean thought of his last shower with Alex, it was the most exhilarating sex he'd had in a long time. Not only that, their separation weighed heavily on his heart and he yearned to see her again. He needed to phone her and decided to do it on the way to the pub. Talking later with a few drinks in him might be considered inappropriate. Brendan, although disgusted they didn't invite him along on the boy's night out, knew they needed time to bond especially now Sean was going away for a while.

Brendan offered to help Claire clean the dishes. She gave a little smile of gratitude; one he had not seen in many years. They had fallen out after Claire left Sean and did not speak much since then, just general chit chat. He could not comprehend why they divorced without making any effort to repair their relationship first.

"You know, I wish it had worked out differently between you and Sean. You were so good together… so in love, what a waste,"

"That's life, Brendan. We did love each other, once, but love fades. We were arguing more than not. It's not a good environment for me, Sean or Kevin. I don't hold anything against him. I still care and that's why I worry that he is making too big a decision, too quickly. I still believe Kevin needs his father,"

"Well, he said it has been on the cards for a while. Going with yer woman is a whole different ball game. He barely knows her. But we can't stop him, he's a grown man and can do what he wants,"
"Like most men, they do what they want,"

"Let's go Kevin. It is midweek and the bar won't be open long."
"Are you off now?" asked Brendan.
"Yes, Dad, see you in a while. We're just going for a few pints and we'll be back soon," said Sean.

"Will you get me a bottle of whiskey in the offy? Here's the money,"

"Kevin can buy it now, he's old enough," Sean giggled.

They left the house waving goodbye. Claire was in deep thought watching her young man walk away. Images of his first step, his first day at school, his first goal and his first girlfriend all came into her mind. What if something had happened to him? How would she have survived without him?

The sun set behind the tall buildings that surrounded them and the air grew cold. Walking side by side, Sean felt relieved and for the first time in a while.

"I'm proud of you, son. You'll do well in your A-levels and go to college. Are you sure you're okay with me going away? If the thought of it upsets you too much, I'll reconsider,"

"Dad, I'll miss you, a lot. I wanna see you happy and if it means travelling with... what's her name?"

"Alex... Alexandra,"

"If travelling with Alex will make you happy, then you go and do that,"

"Thanks Kevin. See, you've even grown up in the past few days," he laughed and comically head-locked his son rubbing his hair with his knuckles.

"Do you mind if I give Alex a quick call? Three minutes, I swear,"

Kevin walked a few paces ahead to allow Sean some privacy on his call. "Hi Alex, how are you doing? I'm fine, thanks. Well, there's a bit of slack from my ex-wife. Ah, she'll be fine. Overwhelmed by the whole lot, I'd say. Kevin? He's coming around, back to a cheeky so and so he was before. So how about you, has there been a follow-up on the 'accident'?"
Sean listened as Alex informed him the Garda had knocked and asked if she knew what Stephen's last actions were. What was his state of mind? What time did they leave him? What happened to the British man who was with them? Yes, they had inquired about Sean. She stuck to the story, although a little different from the Garda Isabelle's account of what Stephen had told her, and they seemed to accept it, for now. Sean was pleased to hear she would not be in trouble with the law.

"Sorry I had to leave you with it. Have you asked about deferring your course?"

Kevin bent down to tie his shoelace and Sean walked by. The streetlights flickered on as the sun slowly departed behind the buildings in the distance.

Alex asked Sean to write down her passport details to book the same flight. He searched through his pockets for a pen and possibly a scrap of paper. An old lady passed by, he stepped back to allow her hunched frame through. She clutched a rickety walking stick, wore a tattered grey coat and had long white shaggy hair covering most of her face. Sean apologised for his open-armed presence on the footpath. Continuing to check all pockets, he felt something in the inside coat pocket he did not remember putting there and pulled it out.

Kevin tried to catch up with his dad. Whilst passing the old lady, she dropped a comb on the ground and he stopped to pick it up.

Sean held the necklace and glanced at Kevin picking up the comb. It dawned on him, the old lady was not who she pretended to be and he had made a big mistake, too big to comprehend.

"No, Kevin. Don't go near her!" he bellowed while running towards them. Alex asked what happened.

"Sean! Sean!" but he had already dropped the phone on the ground.

The crooked lady stood up and leered over Kevin. He screamed for his father. It was too late. Sean desperately tried to reach his son. He would take his place. He would save him. The Banshee shrieked and took Kevin by the scruff of his neck. Kevin pointlessly struggled trying to release himself from her grip. She reached inside his chest and squeezed his heart until it ceased pumping. The blood drained from Kevin's face and he fell limp. She threw him onto the ground and hurried away into the shadows, laughing and pleased her mission was absolute.

Trying CPR, Sean knew it was pointless. Tears flowed down his face. "Kevin, no please. I'm sorry. I forgot the necklace. I'm sorry," he said, kissing Kevin's forehead.
He rocked his son's body back and forth in his arms; from cradle to the grave.

Claire felt a twinge in her heart and held her chest.
"Everything okay?" asked Brendan.
"I don't know Brendan. For a moment there, I didn't feel right."

Made in the USA
Charleston, SC
13 February 2017